Saving
Aunt Alice

For Susan Christine
My thanks to my editor, Glenda Downing,
and to my agent, Margaret Connolly

Random House Pty Ltd
20 Alfred Street, Milsons Point NSW 2061
http://www.randomhouse.com.au

Sydney New York Toronto
London Auckland Johannesburg
and agencies throughout the world

First published in 2001
Copyright © Claire Carmichael 2001

All rights reserved. No part of this publication
may be reproduced, stored in a retrieval system,
or transmitted in any form or by any means,
electronic, mechanical, photocopying, recording
or otherwise, without the prior written permission
of the Publisher.

National Library of Australia
Cataloguing-in-Publication Data

ISBN 1 74051 729 6.

I. Title.

A823.3

Photograph of the author by Reece Scannell.
Cover artwork by Stephen Michael King.
Cover design by Jobi Murphy.
Typeset by Asset Typesetting Pty Ltd in 13/20 Pelham.
Printed by Griffin Press, Adelaide.

Saving Aunt Alice

CLAIRE CARMICHAEL

RANDOM HOUSE AUSTRALIA

PROLOGUE

The little office, doubling as a lab, had an ancient scarred desk sitting next to modern laboratory equipment on white benches. A device hummed quietly in a corner, where a space had been cleared on the dull brown carpet. It was made up of three large loops of glowing green tubing arching over a translucent chair that glowed as though illuminated from within. Attached to one arm of the chair was a small control panel, over which a pattern of coloured lights danced.

Sitting on the chair was a ginger cat. He opened his mouth in a large pink yawn, then blinked his yellow eyes at the woman in her rumpled white lab coat who was peering at a remote control in her hand.

She punched several keys, then said, 'Here goes, Einstein.'

The humming increased, the green tubing glowed brighter. Einstein, in the middle of another pink yawn, disappeared.

She waited a minute or so, then punched keys on the hand control again. A moment passed, then Einstein reappeared. His ears were flattened sideways and he glared at her, obviously displeased. He jumped off the chair and stalked to the door, where he waited, his ginger face full of indignation, to be let out.

Laughing, she opened the door. 'Time travel can't be that bad,' she said to him.

CHAPTER ONE

Tuesday was an awful day for Cal Riddle. It started badly, when he slept in because his mother didn't badger him to get up, as she usually did. Around eight-thirty Cal blinked sleepily at the bedside clock, then shot out of bed as though his pyjamas were on fire.

No time for breakfast. He scrambled into his gym things, stuffed his grey school uniform into a sports bag, and bolted out the door of the apartment, ricocheting off the spindly Mr Olnay, who was moving down the hall like some strange wading bird.

'You're late,' said Mr Olnay in his high, unpleasant voice. The tone was the exact one he used in class when he was criticising some student who didn't get his complicated explanation of a mathematics problem. 'You'd better be on time for *my* class.'

Cal mumbled something and shot out the main entrance of the staff accommodation block. The chill of a winter morning hit him in the face like a slap, and when he took a breath the air stung his lungs. He took a quick look at his watch, groaned, and began to run across the central quadrangle, which was the fastest way to get to the school gymnasium. Mr Chortle, the sports master, had a thing about punctuality, and Cal knew he'd have to be awfully lucky to avoid a detention.

Withering Mansions Coeducational Boarding School looked particularly grand this morning. The imposing, grey buildings, the granite facades still damp from overnight rain, gleamed in the sunlight, and the extensive grounds rolled in green billows to the surrounding sandstone fence. If he'd had time to turn his head, Cal could have seen the huge gates at the bottom of the long drive that greeted visitors with the initials WMCOBS set into the wrought iron in curling, silver letters. From these initials came the school chant, *Wimcobs! Wimcobs! Wimcobs! Withering Mansions Forever!*

Panting, Cal arrived at the gym. In contrast to the main buildings the gym was very modern, sitting like a large white box next to the school sports ground. Cal hurried to the changing room door without much hope. He was right— the door was locked, so he'd have to go in the front way.

Cal paused at the main entrance. He could hear Mr Chortle blowing his whistle, then his irritated voice yelling at someone. Cal tried opening one of the double doors without making too much noise. He'd sneak in and try to join the class without anyone noticing.

Faint hope!

'Well, well,' said Mr Chortle. 'Nice of you to join us, Mr Riddle.'

'Sorry, I'm a bit late.'

Mr Chortle made a big deal of looking at his elaborate three-dial watch while the entire class waited on the basketball court. Cal's friend, Rob Yalta, had a sympathetic expression. The Dimble twins, looking exactly like the bullies they were, sneered.

'A bit late?' said Mr Chortle. 'The class began twenty minutes ago.' He put his fists on his hips. He was short, balding and super-fit. His face was all hard angles, his eyes small and pale blue under heavy brows. 'I'm waiting for an explanation, Riddle.'

'Um … I slept in.'

'Slept in?' repeated Mr Chortle, his voice sarcastic. 'Had a late night, did you?'

The Dimble twins laughed and nudged each other. Rob said something to them and their grins turned to scowls. Rob was a top football player and everyone liked him, even the most bad-tempered of the teachers. Well, almost everyone—the Dimbles didn't, and neither did their friends, the poisonous O'Hara sisters.

'Had a late night, eh?' Mr Chortle repeated.

Cal put his face in neutral. Chortle would just go on and on if he responded. The sports master was hard on everyone, except maybe his daughter Tiffany, but he clearly had a particular grudge against Cal and Cal's mother, Professor Zoe Riddle. Cal had asked his mother why this was so, but every time he did she would hoot with laughter and say Cal wouldn't understand.

The silence stretched. Finally Cal, trying to sound reasonably sincere, said, 'Sorry, sir.'

'Sorry? I'm going to make sure you'll be very sorry. Report to me for detention, first half of lunch.'

The sports master's favourite detention was multiple push-ups, then a brisk run around the oval. Cal didn't mind the thought of running, because he was the school cross-country champion, but he truly hated push-ups, especially when Mr Chortle would be standing beside him making rude remarks about Cal's upper-body strength.

Mr Chortle seized the silver whistle that always seemed to hang around his neck on a chain and blew a shrill blast. 'We've wasted enough time.' He grabbed a basketball and threw it hard at Cal. 'Get going.'

It was fortunate that Cal, although he was only average height, could shoot a basket nine times out of ten, because Mr Chortle was obviously itching to criticise him for something else. After everyone was panting from running from one end of the court to the other, Mr Chortle blew his whistle three times. 'Pathetic!' he yelled. 'Bunch of total no-hopers. Do it again.'

Everyone trooped to the change room at the end of the period. Cal was pulling on his crumpled school uniform while telling Rob how his mother hadn't woken him up on schedule, when one of the Dimbles snatched up one of his gym shoes. Cal made a swipe at it. 'Give that back.'

The Dimble—Cal thought it was Bruce, but he

and George were so like each other it was hard to tell —laughed, shoved Rob out of the way, and lumbered over to the door to lob the shoe into the gym.

There was a bellow of rage from the gym, then Mr Chortle's voice demanding, 'Who threw that?'

A student who'd got changed early came rushing past. Through his laughter he spluttered, 'Great shot! Hit Chortle square on the back of the neck!'

'Hell,' said Rob.

Mr Chortle, his face red, appeared at the doorway, Cal's shoe in his hand. 'Who owns this?' he ground out.

'It's mine,' said Cal, 'but I didn't throw it.'

Rob chimed in, 'He didn't, sir.'

Mr Chortle narrowed his eyes. 'Who *is* responsible?' He glared at Cal. 'Well?'

There was no way Cal could dob anyone in, even if it was a Dimble. And the twins knew it. They stood side by side, their short, pale hair standing up in spikes, their identical high-coloured faces bearing the same smug expression.

Cal said, 'I don't know, sir.'

'I see. Then you have a detention for the entire lunch period, Riddle.'

'But—'

'No buts.' Mr Chortle knew very well that it was against school rules for anyone to spend the whole of lunch in detention. He smiled sarcastically at Cal. 'Yes? Got anything to say?'

Out of the corner of his eye Cal could see the Dimbles grinning. His chest tight with fury, he said, 'I didn't do anything.'

'No? Your shoe mysteriously flies through the air but you see nothing, eh?' Mr Chortle gave him a nasty smile. 'And you know nothing. That sounds about right. Go on, say it out loud, Riddle. "I'm an idiot and I know nothing."'

Before he could prevent it, Cal heard himself say, 'You're an idiot. And you know nothing.'

Somebody gasped. Cal waited with a hollow feeling, silently cursing himself for letting his temper get him into even more trouble. Mr Chortle's face had turned a deeper shade of red.

'That insolence has earned you a third detention, Riddle. After last period of the day, report to me.'

'I've got—'

'You've got what?'

Cal knew that Mr Chortle was well aware there was a school excursion into the nearest town, Wombat Creek, to see a special screening of an action movie. The school bus was leaving straight after the last lesson. Cal had been looking forward to it for days.

Mr Chortle was enjoying himself. 'Anything else smart to say, Riddle? Perhaps you're aiming to get four detentions? I can keep you occupied every moment right up to lights out.'

Cal could hear the Dimbles sniggering together, and a wave of rage almost choked him.

Mr Chortle swung around. 'Who's laughing?' His gaze fell on the Dimble twins. 'Something funny, boys?'

'No, sir,' they said together, the smiles instantly wiped from their faces.

Mr Chortle always insisted students be punctual

for his classes, but he didn't care if they were late for anyone else's, so he spent several minutes lecturing everyone about acceptable behaviour, even though the bell for the next period had sounded.

At last he finished. As Cal passed him in the general rush for the door, Mr Chortle caught his arm. Squeezing until it hurt, the sports master snarled, 'The very beginning of lunch. Be on time.' He shoved his face closer to Cal's. 'And I'll be speaking to your mother about your attitude. I don't imagine she'll be pleased to hear of your behaviour.'

His friend Rob had waited for him. 'Chortle can't give you three detentions like that,' he said as they set off for the main building and their next class.

'Yeah? Just watch him.' Cal's arm throbbed where Mr Chortle had grabbed him. The day couldn't possibly get worse, could it? He had the uneasy feeling that maybe it could.

CHAPTER TWO

On the way to Mr Olnay's maths class Cal and Rob caught up with Jen in the locker room. On Tuesdays Jen's first period was her science class, taught by Cal's mother. Rob was just launching into a description of how Chortle had been hit with one of Cal's shoes, when Cal interrupted him. 'Jen, was my mum there this morning?'

'No,' said Jen, slamming her locker shut. 'Mr Blad took over.'

Cal's skin tingled. He just knew something was

wrong. Only when his mother had something nasty like the flu did she ever miss teaching a class. 'Did Mr Blad say where Mum was?'

Jen gave him a puzzled look. 'He just said that Professor Riddle had been called away. Why?'

Frowning, Rob said, 'What's up? Don't you know where she is?'

'Well … I'm not sure. She wasn't there when I woke up this morning.' Cal shoved his sports bag into his locker and fished around for his mathematics textbook.

'She probably left you a note.'

Jen's suggestion was a good one. He'd skipped breakfast and rushed straight out of the apartment, so it was quite likely a message was sitting on the kitchen counter waiting for him.

The locker room was rapidly clearing as students disappeared into classes. 'Come on, we're going to be really late,' said Jen.

As they hurried along the corridor with other students, Rob said, 'Are you saying that your mother's just gone? Disappeared?'

'Of course not. She must have told me where she was going, and I wasn't listening.'

'Yah, Riddle!' It was a Dimble coming up behind them. 'Hope you like push-ups.' He gave a snort of laughter, elbowed Cal in the ribs, and shoved his way past them.

Rob said something under his breath, but Jen was more direct. 'Oh, it's one of the *Dumb*le twins,' she said in a loud voice.

Someone in the knot of students behind them laughed. The Dimble mumbled something, and disappeared into the classroom. Cal wasn't surprised that Bruce—or was it George—didn't take Jen on, because both the twins had tried it before, and lost out. Jen didn't stand out in a crowd because most of the time she was rather quiet, but she had a great sense of humour and was known for her funny, sharp comments that made people laugh.

In class Cal half-listened as Mr Olnay droned on while scribbling formulae all over the board. Last night Cal's mother had come in to say goodnight the same way she always did. But when he thought about it, somehow it had been different. For one thing, she'd given him a long hug, and that was unusual. For another, she'd forgotten to remind him to floss. Her parents had both been dentists, and she had a real thing about cleaning teeth. She was always buying the latest electric toothbrush and the bathroom had a whole rack of little instruments for massaging gums and removing plaque.

At the end of the period Cal hurried to collect his things. The morning break between periods two and three was fifteen minutes, and he wanted to rush back home and see if the note he hoped to find was there. 'I'll see you in English,' he said to Jen and Rob, and rushed off before they could offer to come with him.

When he entered the apartment he thought his mother must be back, because he had a feeling that someone else was there, but when he called out, no one answered. There was no note on the kitchen bench. He started to check the other rooms, in case she'd put it somewhere else.

Cal was looking through the papers on his mother's bedside table—she often worked on science problems when she couldn't go to sleep —when he thought he heard the soft snick of the front door as if someone had opened or closed it. 'Mum?'

There was no one there. Cal opened the door and looked out into the hallway, but it was empty. He shrugged to himself, feeling a bit stupid to be imagining things.

He tried to convince himself that there was no note from his mother because she was still somewhere in the school doing something or other, but the hollow feeling in his stomach didn't go away. The next best place to check out would be the science department.

The bell to end recess rang as Cal reached the main teaching block, so he knew he'd be late for English. He probably wouldn't be missing much, anyway. There'd been a substitute filling in for their usual teacher, Ms Williamson, who'd managed to break both her legs skiing and wouldn't be back for a month or so. Mr Siddley, the substitute, was a large, flabby man who bleated rather than talked, and had awful problems with discipline, so at the moment English lessons were pretty much a waste of time.

Cal joined the stream of students heading in the direction of the science laboratories. He checked every room, but his mother wasn't to be found. There were two possibilities left—the science staffroom and her private laboratory. As head of the science department she had her own small room, which she had turned into a little lab, and she very often could be found working there. Cal decided to try that first.

By the time he got to the door of her lab lessons had begun and the corridors were deserted except for Einstein, who came strolling along, ginger tail straight up like a flagpole, acting as though he owned the whole establishment. Cal tried the door to his mother's room and found it locked just as Einstein stopped, sat down deliberately, and began to stare at Cal with unblinking yellow eyes.

There wasn't a keyhole to look through because Cal's mother had fitted the door with an electronic lock, opened with a plastic card key. Perhaps she was inside, working, and had locked the door so she wouldn't be disturbed.

Cal knocked and then waited. Einstein tilted his head sideways. Cal thought that if the cat had had eyebrows, he would have raised them in a questioning way.

'I'm looking for Mum,' said Cal, immediately feeling ridiculous that he was explaining something to a ginger cat.

Einstein made a noise that was halfway between a snort and a miaow, got to his feet and stalked away, the very end of his tail flicking irritably. Cal watched him until he disappeared around a corner, then he turned back to the door. He knocked again, then put his ear against the door, hoping to hear something. Maybe she was in there working on some experiment and had forgotten what time it was. There was no sound.

'Just exactly what do you think you're doing,

Calvin? The bell for the next period went some time ago.'

Cal didn't have to turn around to know it was Ms Noreen Hufflet, his biology teacher. Her voice was as sharp as her nose and chin. She dressed very fashionably, had long black hair and a sudden, electric smile that she switched on and off like a light. Cal thought she was a good teacher but very moody, so that she could go from smiles to snarls in the course of one lesson. Right now she was closer to snarling than smiling.

'I'm looking for my mother.'

'When you should be in class? It's something important that's got you wandering around here, is it?'

'Sort of.'

'Sort of isn't good enough,' she snapped. 'Go to your next lesson immediately.'

It was no use arguing with Ms Hufflet when she was in this sort of mood. Cal nodded obediently and set off down the corridor as though he was obeying her instructions. First, though, he'd check the main science staffroom. He was startled to see, as he glanced back over his shoulder, that Ms Hufflet had her head against the door, listening, just as he had been doing a few moments before.

Puzzled, Cal slowed. When he reached the corner he ducked around it and, keeping as much of himself hidden as possible, he watched to see what she was doing.

Just as Cal had, Ms Hufflet tried to open the door. When she had no success, she made an exasperated sound and pushed against the door with her shoulder, at the same time rattling the handle violently. The door remained closed. She stepped back, threw her hands up in a gesture of impatient anger and strode off in the opposite direction, her high heels making a sharp tapping as she went.

Cal wondered why he hadn't heard Ms Hufflet's footsteps earlier when he'd been pressed against the door. Could she have been tiptoeing along, waiting to see if he got into the lab? And why was she so keen to get into his mother's room anyway?

He thought of running after her to ask her, straight out, what was going on. No, that wouldn't work. Not only would she not tell him, in the mood she was in she'd probably give him a detention for insolence, and he had quite enough detentions for today.

Hearing footsteps coming from the direction Ms Hufflet had gone, Cal ducked back behind the corner. The footsteps stopped, and then Cal heard a series of sharp knocks. Showing as little of himself as possible, Cal looked around the corner. Mr Sykes, who was in charge of school security, the cleaning staff and the upkeep of the grounds, was at the door of his mother's room.

He was a wiry little man with a floppy khaki hat that matched his khaki overalls. Under his large, pockmarked nose his droopy grey moustache contrasted with the weather-beaten brick colour of his face.

Mr Sykes knocked again and said, 'Professor Riddle? Are you there?' Then he took a plastic key card out of the pocket of his overalls, slid it into the slot and opened the door. He didn't go in, but put his head into the room. 'Professor Riddle?'

There was a pause, then, mumbling to himself, Mr Sykes shut the door, rattled the handle to make sure it was locked, and went back the way he had come.

Puzzled, Cal watched him go. It was no surprise that Mr Sykes had a key to his mother's room, as he was in charge of security for the school, but why would he be looking for her? And why would he open the door when it was obvious no one was answering his knocking?

CHAPTER THREE

Peering around the door of the science staffroom, Cal saw that it was its usual untidy mess. Most of the teachers' desks were covered with piles of books and papers, and many bits of scientific equipment were shoved into corners or pushed into spots on crammed shelves.

Only one teacher, Morris Blad, was there, his back to the door as he hunched over his overflowing desk. All his attention was on a bright purple folder open in front of him, so he jumped when Cal said, 'Excuse me, I'm looking for my mother.'

Cal caught a quick glimpse of a diagram before Mr Blad hastily closed the folder. 'Did you knock?' he demanded. 'I didn't hear you.'

'Yes, I did. No one answered.' When Mr Blad didn't say anything, Cal went on, 'Have you seen Mum?'

'She isn't here.' Mr Blad's handsome face had a strange, flat expression, as though he was trying to hide what he was thinking. He had long, straight brown hair that flopped over his forehead, and for the last week or so he'd been growing a reddish beard, which was just past the stage of looking as though he'd forgotten to shave.

'Do you know where she might be?' Cal asked. His voice sounded calm, but now Cal was getting seriously worried. 'Jen says you told her class this morning that Mum had been called away.'

Mr Blad tugged gently at his new beard. 'Yes, I did say that. It was just an excuse. I've no idea where Zoe is. I suggest you try the principals.'

'The Witherings?' They'd be the last people to have any idea what was going on, thought Cal, even if Withering Mansions was their own school. 'Do you really think they'll know anything?'

Mr Blad shrugged. He picked up a pile of exercise books and dumped them on top of the purple folder, almost as though he was hiding it from Cal. 'It's worth a try. Now, if you don't mind, I've got some marking to do.'

Cal was going to be very late for English, but that was too bad. He left one fat grey building and headed for an identical one next to it, where the central office of the school was situated. The office was run by Bertha Sykes, a huge woman who was called, but never to her face, Big Bertha. She was married to Burt Sykes, who had just been checking his mother's lab.

It was said that nothing and no one came in or out of the school without Big Bertha knowing all about it. She also made it a point of pride to remember the name of every student in the school, so Cal wasn't surprised when she called out through the sliding glass window of her office, 'Cal Riddle. What do you want?'

Her expression was stern, and her grey hair was screwed up into a tight, disapproving pile on top of her head. She was wearing her usual dark smock, which didn't disguise her weight at all, but made her look like a walking tent. Her blue-framed glasses, attached to their blue plastic chain, rested on her impressive bosom.

'I can't find my mother. Do you know where she is?'

'Have you checked her classrooms?'

'Yes. And the science department. When I got up this morning Mum wasn't there, and I haven't seen her since.'

Big Bertha hated not to have the answer to a question, so Cal was hopeful that she might have some idea of where his mother was.

She frowned. 'Unfortunately, I don't know exactly where your mother might be,' Big Bertha conceded. 'However, I can say, to the best of my knowledge, Professor Riddle has not left Withering Mansions.'

'Would Mr Sykes know something?'

'Burt? Why would my husband be interested in your mother's whereabouts?'

She looked so annoyed that Cal decided it would be wiser not to mention that he'd seen Mr Sykes open the door to his mother's lab. 'I'm a bit worried,' he said, trying to look anxious—which wasn't hard, because he was. 'I don't think Mum would have gone anywhere without telling me.'

Big Bertha's expression softened very slightly. 'I can see why you might be concerned. You'd better speak with the Witherings.' She gestured with one fat hand. 'Down the hall. You know where to go.'

In the hall outside the principals' office Jim Taylor and Kylie O'Hara were on duty at the monitors' table. They were very obviously ignoring each other. This wasn't surprising, because they were sworn enemies. Jim, under-sized but very tough, made up for his lack of height with an aggressive attitude. He was sprawled in his chair, his chin cupped in one hand. Kylie had turned her back to him and was flicking through a magazine.

Even before he got close to the monitors' table, Cal knew she was sniffing. Kylie was allergic to almost everything and carried a box of tissues with her everywhere she went. In class her sniffing could be maddening, especially during a test, when the silence would be broken with sniff, sniff, sniff, and then snuffling noises while she blew her nose.

Cal might have felt sorry for Kylie, except that she and her sister, Fiona, were almost as unpleasant as the Dimbles. Where the Dimbles shoved people around, the O'Hara sisters used hateful words. They delighted in spreading rumours and picking on anyone who could be easily embarrassed or frightened.

Jim sat up when he saw Cal approaching. 'You in trouble?'

Cal didn't blame Jim for his hopeful tone, because it was awfully boring being on monitor duty. Fortunately, they were only rostered on once in a term. In fact, Cal remembered with a groan, that he was on duty that very afternoon.

'Sorry to disappoint you, but no.'

Jim did look disappointed. 'Yeah, well …'

Looking up from the lurid pages of her scandal magazine, the *Trumpheter*, which was specifically banned from the school, Kylie said, 'I was told you *are* in trouble. Big trouble.' She screwed up her face and sneezed, then grabbed a bunch of tissues from the box in front of her and dabbed at her inflamed nostrils. Naturally, then she had to sniff a couple of times. Her sharp face reminded Cal of some pink-nosed rodent.

Looking at Cal with a satisfied smirk, she said, 'I heard you threw a shoe at Chortle in gym this morning.'

'You didn't!' said Jim, plainly thrilled with the idea. 'Wish I'd seen it!'

'It wasn't me.'

Both of them grinned. Jim said, 'Yeah, sure.'

Cal shrugged. He had more important things to worry about. 'I'm here to see the Witherings.'

'Your turn,' said Jim to Kylie.

Snuffling, Kylie got to her feet. 'Suppose I'll have to take you in, then,' she said with a sneer.

 30

She slapped the *Trumpheter* face down on the desk. 'Don't touch it, Taylor,' she warned.

'How'd you get it back from Hufflet?' said Jim. 'I saw her take it from you yesterday.'

Kylie scowled. 'Just keep your hands off it.'

'No risk,' said Jim. 'You've sneezed all over it.'

ALISTAIR AND IVY WITHERING, JOINT PRINCIPALS announced the gold sign on the polished dark wood door. Underneath in smaller letters was the command: *Knock and Enter.*

Kylie ignored the command to knock, and opened the door. As she did so, Ivy Withering's loud voice was saying, '… the boy will have to be told. We can't leave him wondering—'

The voice broke off as Kylie stuck her head around the door. 'Cal Riddle to see you,' she said. Sniffing, she stood aside for Cal to go in, then closed the door behind him. Through the solid wood Cal could hear her furious, 'Give me my *Trumpheter*!' to Jim.

As Cal advanced toward the two identical heavy rosewood desks the principals looked at him with identical expressions of worried surprise. This alarmed Cal immediately. Maybe it was *him* they'd been talking about when Kylie opened the door. And maybe they knew something about what had happened to his mother—and it wasn't good.

Although brother and sister, the Witherings didn't look alike. Alistair Withering was totally bald—the gossip was that he shaved his head every morning. He had a short, chubby body matched by a round face with several double chins. His pale grey eyes were vague and he had a nose that seemed far to small for the rest of him.

He was wearing his usual outfit, a dusty blue suit, rumpled white shirt and a scarlet tie with WMCOBS repeated all over it in navy blue. As red and blue were the official school colours, they were repeated in a banner on the wall behind them.

Alistair Withering's sister, Ivy, was taller, thinner and much louder. She had a horsy face and very large, chalk-white teeth. She was wearing her standard red T-shirt with the words WIMCOBS!

WIMCOBS! WITHERING MANSIONS FOREVER across the front. Cal couldn't see them, but he was sure that below the desk she wore her customary blue shorts and knee-high red socks.

'So, it's you, Cal,' she shouted. It wasn't wise to stand to close to her because she always spoke at full volume. 'Sit down, boy. Sit down.'

'I was looking for my mother, actually.'

A strange look passed between the two Witherings. 'Zoe's been called away,' bellowed Ivy Withering.

As well as being anxious, Cal was starting to get annoyed that he was being kept in the dark. 'Really? She didn't say anything to me.'

'It was sudden,' said Alistair Withering. He had a soft, creaky voice that sounded as if it needed oiling. 'Yes, very sudden. An emergency.'

'An emergency? What sort of emergency?' Cal asked. It couldn't be a problem with a relative because they didn't have any.

Ivy Withering glared at her brother. 'Not an emergency,' she snapped. 'More a minor crisis.'

She switched her attention back to Cal. 'Nothing to worry about.'

'When will she be back?'

His question caused another odd look to pass between brother and sister. 'Not totally sure,' said Alistair Withering. 'Could be hours, could be days. Maybe weeks.'

'*Weeks*?'

'Alistair!' Ivy Withering was clearly furious. 'Think what you're saying, for once.'

'Not months,' said her brother, showing his teeth in what he seemed to think was a reassuring smile. 'My guess is that she'll be back any moment now.'

'You don't have to eat with the other students in the school dining hall,' said Ivy Withering. 'You must have your meals with us. And you can stay with us too, if you like.' She was becoming enthusiastic. 'The attic would be perfect for you. Perfect!'

The thought of staying in Withering House, built as a tiny replica of the main school, was not appealing. Not only did the Witherings not believe in heating, even in winter, they also refused to have a television set. And on top of that, they were also strict vegetarians and ate practically everything raw.

'I'll be okay,' said Cal. 'Really. I mean, there's plenty of food in the fridge.'

Alistair Withering frowned. 'Meat?' he asked. 'Are there red meat products in your refrigerator?'

Cal felt a lecture coming on. 'Maybe ...' he said vaguely.

'Tsk!' Alistair Withering shook his shiny head. 'Your mother just won't listen. I've told Zoe a thousand times that red meat is poison. A growing boy being exposed to those toxins ...' His creaky voice trailed off as he shook his head again.

The menu for the school dining hall included white meat dishes, due to parent and student pressure, but no red meat of any kind was permitted to be served. This meant that every time anyone went to town, they made a beeline for McDonald's for hamburgers.

Ivy Withering stood up, smiling. Above her large

white teeth she exposed an expanse of glistening pink gum. 'When we hear from Zoe, you'll be the first to know. In the meantime, if there's anything you need, do come to us immediately.'

'Cal's going to be late for his English class,' said Alistair with a meaningful glance at his sister. 'Perhaps, under the circumstances ...' He let his voice trail off as he tilted his head in an unspoken question.

Astonished that the principal should actually know which class he was missing, Cal said, 'Could I have a late pass for English, please?' Frankly, he thought that Mr Siddley, the substitute teacher, would be more than happy to have one less student in the class.

Another look passed between the Witherings. 'How would you like it,' said Ivy Withering, 'if I arranged for you to be excused for the entire lesson? In fact, it would be an excellent idea if you went back home, just in case Zoe calls.'

'Is Mum likely to call?'

'I think it highly unlikely,' Alistair began. He

stopped as his sister shot him a look so hot with rage that Cal thought it surprising it didn't bore a hole right through his head. 'Ah ...' Alistair Withering said. He stopped and cleared his throat. 'That is, Cal, there's always a possibility your mother might call.'

'Better safe than sorry,' Ivy Withering shouted. 'I suggest you stay in the apartment at least until lunchtime. That way we'll know where to find you if we hear anything.'

Cal didn't point out that they would know where to find him if he was in class, too. Willing to go along with this suspicious niceness, he said, 'Okay, thanks.'

'One of the monitors will take a note to your English teacher.'

As Cal left the office he looked back over his shoulder. It was odd how they were staring at him: Alistair with a troubled face, Ivy with an expression that could almost be pity.

CHAPTER FOUR

Cal had spent his time in the apartment looking for a spare electronic key to his mother's lab, but hadn't been able to locate it. He knew she wasn't in the lab, because Mr Sykes had opened the door and checked, but Cal thought maybe there'd be some clue about where she'd gone—perhaps an appointment book, or a note, or something. He could always ask Mr Sykes to open the door for him, but that would mean getting permission from the Witherings, and Cal had the disturbing feeling they were hiding something from him, and probably wouldn't let him in the room anyway.

There was no message for him on the answering machine, and he didn't want to hang around waiting for something to happen. Deciding to meet up with his friends, he timed it so he'd meet Jen and Rob outside the classroom just after the English period ended.

'Your aunt is *weird*!' said Jen the moment she saw him.

Cal stared at her. 'I don't have an aunt.'

'She says she's your aunt.'

'Who does?'

'Ms Roid, the new English teacher.' Jen looked at Rob for support. 'Rob'll tell you.'

'This is stupid,' said Cal, convinced his friends were playing a trick on him.

Rob grinned. 'Well, she said her name was Alice Roid and that she was Cal Riddle's aunt.' He poked Cal in the chest. 'And that's you.'

'She was disappointed when you weren't there,' added Jen, very amused. 'And you should have heard the Dimbles at the back of the class laughing about her.'

'Yeah. Until she shut them up.'

Whoever this new teacher was, Cal had to admit that shutting up the Dimble twins was quite an achievement. 'Who is she really?' he said.

'Your aunt,' they said together.

Cal looked at them, exasperated. 'But I don't *have* an aunt. I've never had one. I don't even have an uncle or a cousin.'

'Good thing,' said Jen. 'I wouldn't want a relative like Ms Roid.' She glanced over Cal's shoulder. 'Here she comes. You can see for yourself.'

Cal turned to see an extraordinary woman coming out of the classroom. Tall and angular, she had piercing dark eyes with curved black eyebrows like two semicircles, a jutting hooked nose and an odd, rectangular mouth. Her wildly tangled hair was a peculiar reddish colour, and she wore a bright yellow blouse and lime-green skirt. There was a deep purple scarf around her neck and shocking pink shoes on her large feet.

Before she reached them, Alistair Withering, his red tie flapping over his shoulder, came galloping around the corner. He skidded to a stop and wheezed, 'You were supposed to stay at home, Cal.'

His face quite pink from rushing, he tried to catch his breath. It was obvious he had something more to say, but before he could speak, his sister, her bony knees pumping, came speeding up to them. 'Ah!' she yelled. 'Here you are, Cal. I see you've met your Aunt Alice.'

Cal was convinced that he had never seen this peculiar woman before in his life. 'I'm sorry, I don't have an Aunt Alice.'

He could hear Rob and Jen whispering behind him. Apparently Ivy Withering could hear them too, because she barked, 'You! Yes, you—the boy and girl there. Off to your next class, and don't dawdle.'

With several backward glances, Cal's two grinning friends went slowly off down the corridor. Several other students stopped to see what was going on, until Ivy Withering glared at them, and then they reluctantly moved away.

'You have grown up,' the strange woman said to Cal. She had a grating, metallic voice. 'You were a little boy when I saw you last.'

Sure that he would never forget someone who looked like this eccentric woman, Cal said, 'I don't remember you.'

Ivy Withering patted his shoulder with a heavy hand. 'Of course you do. This is your father's sister.'

Cal's heart jumped. His father had been gone for many years, but he still had a vague impression of a big man with a deep, warm voice. 'You knew my dad?'

After one of her loud, whooping laughs, which made everyone stare at her, Ivy Withering announced, 'Of course your aunt knows your father. He's her brother, isn't he?'

The principal was talking as though his father were still alive. With sudden hope, Cal said to his never-before-known aunt, 'When did you last see him?'

Alistair Withering waved his hands around so wildly that Cal stared at him, astonished. The principal was always very calm, and spoke in a soft voice, but here he was, looking like he was about to take off and fly. 'You must talk with your aunt, in private, immediately!'

'Oh, okay,' said Cal, wondering why it was so urgent.

Alistair Withering looked as though he was going to say something else, but his sister stared intensely at him until he shut his mouth. She turned to Cal with a smile that seemed pasted on her long face. 'While your mother's away, your aunt will be staying in the apartment with you. It'll be such fun for you.'

Aunt Alice's rectangular mouth stretched wide in a smile, revealing many small, even teeth. 'That will be nice.' She abruptly stepped forward to put her long, thin arms around him and squeezed him in a hug. 'I am feeling affection for my nephew. We will spend quality time together.'

Quality time? Cal felt as though he were being squeezed to death. 'Gaaagh!' was the only sound he could make.

Aunt Alice promptly released him. 'Oh. Too tight,' she said.

'A bit,' gasped Cal, trying to get his breath back.

'You must take the next period off and settle your aunt into the apartment,' said Ivy Withering in a tone that would not be disobeyed. 'I'll advise your teacher myself.'

Next period was biology with Ms Hufflet, and there was a test, so Cal didn't mind missing the class at all . He supposed he'd better try being a bit helpful, so he said to the woman claiming to be his aunt, 'Where's your luggage?'

Aunt Alice, whoever she was, seemed puzzled. 'Luggage?'

'Your aunt's travelling light,' said Ivy Withering. 'She only brought an overnight bag with her.'

Aunt Alice's semicircular eyebrows shot up. 'Ah, yes, the bag. I left it in the office of Professor Riddle.' She looped an arm around Cal's shoulders. 'We shall go there now.'

Watched by the Witherings, they set out together. Cal wriggled out from under the weight of her arm and positioned himself so she couldn't try hugging him again. He looked sideways at his so-called aunt as they walked through crowds of students making their way to their next classes. She looked odd, she sounded odd, and she was calling his mother Professor Riddle as though they had never met each other. There was no way Cal wanted to be related to this woman.

'About my dad—'

'Later, when we can speak privately.'

She was darting quick glances in all directions, as though expecting any moment to be attacked. Great, he thought. She's not only odd to look at, she's probably off her rocker too.

When they reached the building where his mother's room was, Cal said, 'How did you get into Mum's lab? The door was locked.'

Aunt Alice's eyebrows slid down until they almost touched her black eyes. 'Of course it was locked. There is something extremely valuable in the room. Security is vital.'

Cal couldn't think of anything in his mother's

lab that would be worth much money, but he wasn't going to argue with this woman. 'When I was looking for Mum I tried to get in, but I couldn't,' he said. 'Do you have a key?'

Aunt Alice pushed out her thin lips while she stared at him. 'In a way,' she said at last.

Out of the corner of his eye Cal could see that his companion was making quite an impression. Some students were pointing and making remarks, others were straight out gaping. Before this moment Cal had been sorry he didn't have aunts and uncles and cousins like most people, but this relative was way too embarrassing.

Worse, he could see the O'Hara sisters, sniffing Kylie and sharp-tongued Fiona, approaching. They caught sight of Cal and Aunt Alice, and speeded up, laughing and pointing as they got closer. Any moment now Fiona would say something really nasty, and Cal didn't think it was anything his aunt should have to deal with, even if she *was* the weirdest person he'd ever met.

'We'd better hurry,' he said. If he was stuck with

this unusual aunt, he didn't want the whole school staring at them both. The sooner he could get her out of sight, the better.

'These two girls cause trouble?' said Aunt Alice, pointing at the O'Haras with one very skinny finger.

'Sort of.'

'Sort of? That's not an adequate reply.' She abruptly halted and stared hard at the O'Hara sisters. The girls stopped laughing, then changed direction and ducked into the nearest classroom.

'I recognise the type,' Aunt Alice said. 'They enjoy bullying weaker people.'

Cal looked at her with new respect. 'That's about it.'

'And I wouldn't be surprised to find they had criminal tendencies.'

'I don't know about that ...'

Aunt Alice gave him a grim little smile. 'I am feeling pleasure at the thought that perhaps they will be students in one of my English classes. I would like that.'

Cal thought he might like it too. 'You'll be

teaching them in Drama. I'm in the same class, but it's not until next week.'

Rubbing her hands together with a rasping sound, Aunt Alice said, 'Excellent. I am skilled in Drama, especially the works of Egmont Ellis Gluttop.'

'Who?'

'You've never heard of Egmont Ellis Gluttop?' asked Aunt Alice, clearly outraged. 'Why, he's one of the—' She broke off and her face turned a faint pink. 'I am feeling embarrassment,' she said. 'Of course, he isn't born yet.'

'What?'

'Oh, nothing. Now, quickly, we must hurry to your mother's laboratory.'

Cal was ahead of Aunt Alice when they reached the lab, so he turned the knob of the door to show that it was locked. 'See, it won't open.'

He stood aside for her to try. She put one long-fingered hand on the handle and waited for a moment, then opened the door. Astonished, Cal said, 'How did you do that?'

'The door was stuck.'

Cal knew that wasn't true, but she hadn't used a key card to get in. What was going on?

Inside the room, Cal looked around. There was an open folder on the battered desk, a half-eaten apple next to it, and a mug half full of cold coffee. Cal quickly checked the desk, but there was no appointment book, nor any note that gave a clue where his mother might have gone.

He looked over at his aunt, who was staring at one corner of the room, her curved eyebrows hovering near her hairline. Cal couldn't work out why she was so surprised.

'What's the matter?' he said.

'The matter? It has gone. Someone has removed it.' Aunt Alice swivelled her head to look into Cal's face. 'I am feeling dismay and dread,' she said. 'This is a dreadful blow.' She switched her gaze back to the empty corner. 'And how terribly unfortunate for Professor Zoe Riddle.'

CHAPTER FIVE

'What do you mean, a dreadful blow? What's missing?' Cal knew he sounded sharp, even rude, but he didn't care. 'Are you talking about your overnight bag? Has somebody taken it? Are you expecting Mum to pay for it?'

'Bag?'

'Your *luggage*!' Cal didn't bother to hide his impatience. 'We came here to get your clothes and things, remember?'

Looking around the room, he found a bulging overnight bag shoved under a laboratory bench. 'Is this it?' he said, picking the bag up to show her.

The bag was made of an inky-black soft plastic, and had two stout handles but no discernable opening. Aunt Alice inspected it closely. 'Yes. That is mine, but I left it beside the desk.'

Cal watched her as she went over to the corner she'd been staring at and knelt down. Her narrow bottom in the air and her nose almost touching the dusty brown carpet, she said, 'If you care to look, you can see the indentations in the carpet where it was placed. It has definitely been removed.'

'Been removed?' With a flash of irritation, Cal realised he was starting to repeat things the same way this odd-looking woman did. 'If something's missing we'd better tell the Witherings.'

His aunt turned her head abruptly, staring up at him with her unfathomable eyes. Then she unfolded herself from her kneeling position and stood up 'No. Take me to the apartment, now, please.'

Cal didn't come to his mother's room often, and

even when he concentrated hard he couldn't think what had been in that particular corner. The place was full of so many bits and pieces, many of them odd looking, that whatever had been sitting there had fitted right in with everything else. 'What exactly is it that's disappeared?' he asked.

Aunt Alice was already striding out the door, her overnight bag swinging from one angular hand. 'I will advise you of everything. Soon. Now, take me to the apartment of your mother.'

Trying to make up for his rude tone when Aunt Alice had annoyed him so much in his mother's lab, Cal decided to be as pleasant as possible. 'This is the living room,' he said as soon as they were through the front door.

Cal took her overnight bag from her and put it on the pea-green couch. He picked up a music magazine he'd dropped on the floor the night before. 'Sorry. It's a bit of a mess.'

His aunt put out her hand. 'I would like to see that.' She flicked through the pages, pausing to peer at things that obviously caught her interest. 'Interesting,' she said, handing it back to him. 'A very good example of out-dated technology. Quite fascinating.'

Hands on hips, she surveyed the room. 'What sort of security measures do you have?'

'It's quite safe here, you know.'

She didn't seem reassured. 'Safe? I think not. I am feeling disquiet. Please show me every room.'

'Okay. The kitchen's over here.'

She followed him, her glance darting everywhere as though she expected something to leap out at her. Of course, nothing did, although Cal did remember the odd feeling he'd had in the apartment earlier, as though someone had been there with him.

Guessing that his aunt would want to eat at home with him, rather than go to the school dining hall and be ogled by all the Withering Mansions boarders, he opened the freezer compartment of the refrigerator to see what was available.

'There's macaroni and cheese,' he said. 'Mum

always calls it comfort food. I can cook that in the microwave for tonight, no trouble.'

Aunt Alice's eyebrows rose. She reached past him and took the frozen dinner from the freezer. Turning it in her bony hands, she read every word on the packet. 'Salt, artificial colours, artificial flavours, bleached flour?' Her eyebrows fell into a frown. 'You eat this?'

'Of course, everybody does.'

She gave a disapproving grunt. 'Extraordinary.'

'Does that mean you don't want it for dinner?'

'I will not be eating.'

'Okay.' Well, he would be. He hadn't had any breakfast and he was hungry.

When they got to his mother's room, Cal said, 'I'll change the sheets on Mum's bed for you.'

'What for?'

He looked at her, surprised. 'Because that's where you'll be sleeping.'

'I will not be sleeping.'

This was getting too weird. Cal folded his arms. 'I don't suppose you'll be having a shower, either.'

'A shower will not be necessary.'

Ignoring Cal, Aunt Alice began to go over the whole apartment again, this time her gaze closely scanning the walls, ceilings and floor. Coming back to the living room, she went to the window and carefully examined the ground outside. Then she went to the front door of the apartment and put her ear against it.

'Aunt Alice—'

He was silenced by her impatient gesture. At last she said, 'We are not under surveillance at the moment.'

Oh, great. It wasn't enough that she looked totally peculiar, she was totally insane too. 'That's good,' he said in a calming voice.

She swung around to fix him with a compelling gaze. 'I have something important to tell you. A message from your mother.'

'From Mum? Where is she? When will she be home?'

His questions gained a snort from his aunt. 'I am feeling what I would call regretful amusement,' she

said. 'You have asked the zillion-dollar question.'
She shook her head slowly, repeating, 'When will
she be home …'

'When *will* she?'

'A sad but somewhat humorous question.'

'What's so funny?'

'What is funny, Cal, is that your mother can't
get home. Professor Riddle is stuck seventy years
into the future, and she cannot get back. And
worse—it is apparent that someone is making sure
that she never does.'

CHAPTER SIX

Cal felt as though he'd been hit on the head. Hard. He realised his mouth was hanging open, and he closed it so quickly that he bit his tongue. At last he managed to say, 'This is a joke, right?'

One of Aunt Alice's eyebrows went up while the other went down. 'It is not a joke. I am telling you the precise truth. Professor Zoe Riddle—who, incidentally, is quite famous in the future as a pioneer time traveller—has been caught seventy years from now because her quantum time machine will not work. She has sent me from the future to fix the problem.'

He felt as though a thick fog was filling his head. 'I don't believe this.'

She lifted her narrow shoulders in a neat shrug. 'You may believe or not believe, whichever you choose, but I assure you that your mother has sent me to your rather primitive era to find out what has gone wrong.'

The fog in Cal's brain was joined by a dizzy feeling. He shook his head to clear it. 'Why did Mum go in the first place, if she knew she couldn't get back?'

Speaking slowly, as if to someone especially dumb, Aunt Alice said, 'Your mother is a scientist, and knows that risks must be taken to achieve advances in technology. She had no reason to worry, as the time machine had worked perfectly on a number of trial runs.'

Suddenly resentful, Cal said, 'Mum didn't tell me anything about these experiments. She shouldn't have tried time travel if she thought there was a chance she couldn't come back.'

He was learning that Aunt Alice had very little patience. She gave an irritated sigh, then said, 'I have already explained that the machine showed no signs of trouble, otherwise your mother would not have risked this particular trip into the future to find your father. However, during this last experiment something went very wrong. Put simply, the time machine has developed a serious fault in its quantum reversal circuits.'

'My dad!' exclaimed Cal. 'What about my dad?'

'Please calm yourself,' snapped Aunt Alice, her semicircular eyebrows pushed together in a frown. 'You were very young, a mere baby, when your father disappeared in an early time travel experiment. The machine unfortunately blew itself to pieces before he could get back. For many years your mother has been building a new time machine so that she can rescue your father from the future.'

Cal stared at her, thinking this could not possibly be true. Okay, he'd play along with this madwoman and listen to what else she had to say. 'Mum is stuck in the future with Dad. Is that right?'

'No. In fact they are marooned in different time periods. Your father is, I believe, possibly ninety years into the future. Professor Zoe Riddle unfortunately made a miscalculation when she set the time parameters for this latest experiment at seventy years into the future.'

Cal felt he was beyond being surprised by anything this astonishing woman could say. Acting as though he believed every word of her incredible story, he said, 'So Mum's time machine broke. Can't she fix it?'

'The time machine that remains here is the one that must be repaired. The replica that was shifted in time carrying your mother can only accomplish a reverse time shift if the one in her laboratory is working perfectly.'

Sure that he had caught Aunt Alice in a lie, Cal said triumphantly, 'You say Mum sent you from the future, but if the time machine won't work, how come you could use it to get here?'

Hands on his hips, he waited for Aunt Alice's reply.

She was showing no signs that his question had caught her out. 'You will not understand any of the technology,' she said. 'However, put very simply, the time machine has developed a serious fault in its quantum reversal circuits. This fault means that it cannot time-shift living beings.'

Cal gave a scornful laugh. 'And I suppose you're telling me you're dead, so it can time-shift you.'

'Your mother cannot return to this particular time and place because she is composed of flesh and blood. I am not.'

Aunt Alice bent to look closely into his face. 'My superior programming enables me to read human body language efficiently. I deduce that you are puzzled.' Aunt Alice put up one hand and snatched her red wig from her head. 'You see?'

Her skull shone with a dull metallic sheen. Cal could see several indentations and a couple of small trapdoors. He realised his mouth was hanging open again.

'I am, in fact, a Supreme Deluxe Android, Type SD24.' She put her other hand up to her right ear and gave it a hard pull. There was a click, and her face swung forward like a hinged door. Cal could see the inside of her skull was packed with glowing circuits. Without her face to surround them, her black eyes stared at him from the end of two stalks.

'Whoa!' said Cal, sitting down suddenly.

Aunt Alice snapped her face back into place and plonked the red wig back on her head. 'Did I mention that the *SD* designation indicates that I am the Super Deluxe model?'

Her expression made it clear that Cal was supposed to be impressed. 'I'm sure that's very good,' he said, his voice very faint.

Forming her letterbox mouth into a proud smile, Aunt Alice said, 'So you understand, I am not your Aunt Alice, although I do appear to be a totally convincing member of your family.'

Totally convincing? Even at this moment, Cal couldn't stop a snort of amusement.

'What is so amusing?' demanded Aunt Alice.

Although very tempted to say, 'Actually, *you* are!' Cal managed instead to comment, 'Well, you do look a bit strange.'

Aunt Alice, frowning, glanced down at herself. 'Strange? I researched your historical period extensively, and I determined that my present appearance would be very appropriate.'

She sounded hurt, and Cal was instantly sorry. 'What I mean is, your clothes are … uh, rather bright.'

This was an understatement: her lime-green skirt almost glowed, her blouse was a brilliant yellow and her purple scarf was that particular hectic shade that hurt Cal's eyes. Add to that her red wig and pink shoes, and she was an unforgettable sight.

Aunt Alice took his remark as a compliment. 'I do like distinct colours,' she said in a pleased tone. 'Professor Riddle suggested something a little less bright would do, but the final decision on clothes was mine, and I believe I fit in well.'

'What made you pick the red wig?' asked Cal,

hiding a grin because it was on crooked, and was sliding off over her left ear.

'You like it? I thought it went well with my outfit.' She indicated her overnight bag. 'I have more early twenty-first century clothes in there. I'm sure you'll like them too. Also, I have a written message from Professor Riddle.'

A message? Could that be true? He looked at the overnight bag sitting on the couch. 'Can I see the message, please?'

Aunt Alice had caught sight of herself in the wall mirror near the front door and was tut-tutting loudly. 'You should have told me my hair was not correctly positioned.'

'Mum's message—can I see it, please?'

'In a moment.' She made quick adjustments to her wig. 'No one must suspect that I am anything but your Aunt Alice.' She swung around to look at him intently. 'You understand? It is vital, absolutely vital that no one realises that I am an android. If that happens, my mission is not likely to be completed.'

Perhaps he was going mad, but Cal was beginning to believe that this strange creature was exactly what she said she was. 'And your mission is to fix the time machine?' he asked.

Her semicircular eyebrows tilted into a heavy frown. 'My mission is to return your mother to her own time. This would not be a difficult task, if her time machine were available. Unfortunately, it is a scientific law of time travel that you must return in the machine that sent you, a law that is making it very hard for your mother to rescue your father, as she needs to speak with him before she can build an exact replica of his original machine, which exploded after he had travelled forward in time.'

'So the first thing is to find Mum's time machine.'

Aunt Alice nodded. 'Precisely. Someone has absconded with the device, and hidden it some-where in the school.'

'But who would know Mum had a time machine?'

Aunt Alice pursed her lips, making her mouth

into an off-centre O shape. 'Your mother has enemies,' she said at last. 'I have no knowledge of who they might be, but Professor Riddle is sure that it is no accident that the machine malfunctioned.'

Cal pictured Aunt Alice on her hands and knees in his mother's office, her bottom in the air as she inspected the carpet. 'Are you sure you're not mistaken about where the time machine was when you saw it? Maybe you didn't look in the right place.'

Aunt Alice waved her arms around, simultaneously jigging up and down. 'I have been programmed with the full range of emotions,' she announced. 'At this moment I am very agitated. It is disturbing. Very disturbing. My mission must be completed. I have made no mistake. The time machine should be in the corner of your mother's laboratory.'

Abruptly, she stopped jigging. 'Ah-hah!' she said, her eyebrows shooting up her forehead. 'At this moment I am experiencing hope at the possibility that the time machine has been moved to another part of the laboratory and I overlooked it. When we were there you didn't see it, did you?'

Cal spread his hands. 'I don't have the faintest idea what it looks like.'

Aunt Alice's straight mouth bent down at the corners. 'You have no concept of a time machine?' She took two big strides over to the fat overnight bag and ran a forefinger along the top. Immediately, it peeled open to reveal a clashing mixture of brightly coloured clothes. She rummaged around and finally handed him a hand computer. 'Your mother has detailed everything here.'

Cal took the little computer and activated it. Instantly, a message appeared on its glowing screen.

My dear Cal, you are reading this because something has gone very wrong with my time travel plans. I am attempting to send an android back to our era to repair my time machine. She will be disguised as a relative, Aunt Alice. She will go to the Witherings and explain what has happened. No one else must know anything about this.

Aunt Alice, who'd been reading over Cal's shoulder, pointed with one thin finger as he scrolled down the screen. 'There is a diagram of your mother's time machine. In real life it's a delightful bright green.'

Cal frowned at the diagram, which didn't look like anything more than a few loops of tubing arranged over a chair-like object. Underneath the diagram were the words, THE RIDDLE TEMPORAL SHIFTER.

'This is a time machine?' he said doubtfully. 'I didn't see anything like this in Mum's lab.' He frowned, remembering that he'd seen a similar diagram somewhere else.

'More accurately, as it says below the diagram, a temporal shifter,' said Aunt Alice. 'Ah!' Her finger stabbed at the little screen. 'And here we have my specifications. You will see that I am indeed a Supreme Deluxe Android.'

She sounded so self-important that Cal couldn't resist teasing her. 'And you're saying that's good, are you?' he said with a grin.

'Your tone is causing me to feel indignation,' declared Aunt Alice. 'I must inform you that I have the most subtle androidian refinements. Not only do I have the correct body heat for a human, my skin can change colour, so I am able to go white with shock, or red with rage. I am programmed with the full range of human emotions.'

Cal tried to stop smiling. 'Oh, really?' he said.

Aunt Alice's eyebrows descended into a heavy frown as she glared at him. 'The full range,' she repeated, then added, 'At this moment I am changing from indignation to feelings of irritation and a touch of bitterness.'

'Sorry,' said Cal. 'I can see you're perfect for the job.' He couldn't help thinking that it would have been better if Aunt Alice had been a quiet little android, wearing dull colours and having a less eye-blinking shade of hair.

'Yes, I *am* the ideal choice,' Aunt Alice agreed, 'particularly as there is a mystery regarding the whereabouts of the time machine.' Her expression smug, she went on, 'You see, I have been programmed with the detective arts.'

'The detective *arts*?'

'Don't repeat me, please. I find it aggravating.'

'Sorry.'

Aunt Alice, her voice full of pride, went on, 'Not only have I been fully programmed with the detective arts, I am also equipped with the time machine repair skills, the entire range of human emotions, including a sense of humour, and in preparation for my role as a member of the staff of Withering Mansions, the full English syllabus.' She paused. 'And, of course, my teaching credentials include advanced Koga.'

Cal blinked. 'Koga? We don't have any subject like that. What is it?'

'You do not have Koga?' Aunt Alice's expression clearly showed her embarrassment. 'I believed I had researched your period very diligently, but if Koga hasn't been developed yet …'

She shook her head so hard her wig threatened to fly off. 'I am sure Koga comes into use in classrooms in your time period. Perhaps Withering Mansions is slow to adopt new teaching techniques.'

'So what is this Koga thing?'

She made a dismissive gesture. 'It is impossible to explain, but when you experience Koga you will recognise it immediately.'

Suddenly she grabbed his elbow in a paralysing grip.

'Ow! What's that for?'

'Be quiet!' She tilted her head, seeming to listen to something Cal couldn't hear. 'I am detecting electromagnetic waves. Surveillance of the apartment is beginning. We can speak no further.'

'But—'

Aunt Alice silenced him with a glare. 'My mission is to return your mother to this time. I must find, and repair, the quantum time machine. No one must have any suspicion that I am from the future. I rely on you to help me.'

Just as suddenly as she had grabbed him, Aunt Alice released his elbow. 'Oh,' she said, her face going slightly pink, 'I am in error. We are not under surveillance. I believe someone is using a microwave device in one of the other apartments.'

The mention of a microwave reminded Cal that his stomach was empty. In his mind's eye he could see the macaroni and cheese steaming on a plate. 'I'll just get something to eat—'

'Eat? There's no time to waste! Doesn't Professor Riddle make that very clear in her message to you?'

Cal looked down at the tiny screen in his hand. The last words his mother had written were in pulsating red:

I suspect that someone at Withering Mansions does not want me to return. I don't know who it is, but be very careful, Cal. Aunt Alice is to repair the machine as soon as she can. It is vital that no one suspects anything. You must do everything you can to save Aunt Alice from exposure as an artificial being.

Cal looked over at his android aunt, noticing that her red wig was slipping off backwards this time. He shook his head. Saving Aunt Alice was going to be a real challenge.

CHAPTER SEVEN

Cal had got Aunt Alice to adjust her wig, and they were about to leave the apartment when a loud siren sounded one long blast, followed by three shorter blasts.

Aunt Alice grabbed Cal's elbow again. 'What is that! A disaster alarm?'

He wrenched his elbow away from her. 'It's the signal for a special school assembly. Everyone has to go to the central quadrangle as soon as they hear it.'

'Indeed? Then we'd better hurry.' Aunt Alice radiated enthusiasm. 'This could be most interesting. I have not attended a special school assembly before.'

They joined the crowds of students and teachers pouring out of the buildings and heading for the quad. Cal checked Aunt Alice out of the corner of his eye. She was striding along, her glance, as usual, darting everywhere. He could hear murmured comments, and it wasn't hard to imagine what people were saying. She certainly didn't look like a machine—her skin was very realistic and her movements quite natural, but she did make an unusual human being.

The Witherings, both with grave expressions, were already standing on the steps overlooking the quadrangle. Ignoring the cold, Ivy Withering's arms and skinny legs were bare. 'Hurry along,' she shouted, not needing a microphone for amplification. 'This is a very serious matter.'

Cal's stomach turned over. It couldn't be about his mother, could it? With sudden relief he realised that he would have been told first, so it must be about something else. 'You have to stand with the teachers,' he said to his aunt.

'Ah!' Aunt Alice was delighted. 'Stand with the teachers. I will be making conversations.'

'No, you won't,' said Cal, grabbing her arm. 'You can't talk when an assembly is on. You have to listen.'

'I am keen to use my conversational abilities.'

'Well you can't. Not right now, anyway,' he said.

Aunt Alice, looking disappointed, went over to join a group of teachers. Cal found his roll class and attached himself to the end of a line, waving to Jen, who was down the other end with Rob.

When everyone was in place, Ivy Withering shouted, 'Absolute quiet, please!'

Alistair Withering's creaky voice did need a microphone to be heard. Bundled up in an overcoat, he looked mournfully over the assembly, his bald head shining in the weak sunlight. 'It is with deep regret,' he began, 'that I must tell you that we have a thief in the school.'

Waiting until the murmuring died down, he went on, 'A teacher's belongings have been rifled. The person responsible entered an empty staffroom and took the opportunity to steal items of value.'

He shook his head. 'This is not the Withering Mansions tradition. We do not steal from each other. No, we maintain the highest of personal standards.'

After a long pause, he said, 'Now, my sister and I ask for the guilty party to please step forward. This is the honorable thing to do.'

No one moved.

Ivy Withering seized the microphone and deafened everyone by bellowing, 'Own up now or suffer the consequences! We will find you, whoever you are!'

No one moved.

'Very well,' yelled Ivy Withering, 'this assembly is over, but be very sure our investigations will continue.'

The bell sounded to indicate that it was officially lunchtime. As everyone, chattering loudly, began to move away, Cal checked his watch. The period before lunch had ended early to fit in the assembly, so if he hurried, he'd be on time for the first of his three detentions with Mr Chortle. First, however, he'd better see what Aunt Alice was up to.

'Can't talk,' he said to Jen, who had her mouth open ready to ask him something. 'I've got that detention with Chortle. And one after school, too.'

'You'll be missing the movie at Wombat Creek.'

'Yeah, I know.'

Most people had moved off already, but Aunt Alice was hovering near a couple of teachers who were deep in conversation, her head tilted toward them and her lips pressed together. Cal pulled her away, and asked, 'What are you doing, Aunt Alice?'

'As you suggested, I am listening. What member of staff is Noreen?'

'That would be Ms Hufflet. She's a biology teacher.'

Aunt Alice nodded knowingly. 'That is what I

was overhearing. Someone called Noreen is the victim of the robbery. Things were taken from her handbag, which was in a drawer of her desk.'

Cal checked his watch again. 'I've got to go. Will you be all right?'

'I will make conversations with teachers and school staff,' she declared. 'I will utilise my sense of humour whenever possible. This friendly chatting will enable me to form opinions about which one is responsible for stealing the time machine.'

'What will you be chatting about?' asked Cal.

Aunt Alice's smile faded. 'I have not been specifically programmed for chatting.'

Cal realised he was going to be late for Chortle's detention if he didn't speed up right now. 'The weather,' he said hastily. 'People often chat about the weather. It's a safe topic.'

'The weather? Is that the only suitable subject?'

Cal didn't dare suggest she discuss cricket or football, she'd probably start giving statistics for the future seventy years, so he said, 'People are interested in different things, you can always let them talk about things they like.' He frowned at her. 'And you just nod, and say, "Really?" and things like that. Do you understand?'

'Of course I understand!' Aunt Alice was beaming again. 'I will see you later today to report my progress.'

His last glimpse of his Aunt Alice showed that at least her wig was on straight, but Cal thought she still looked as though she'd just landed from another planet—which in a way, she had.

As he hurried past clumps of students heading for the dining hall, Cal's thoughts were bouncing around inside his head. His mother had always said that his father had gone away and might be back one day, but as the years passed Cal had become convinced there was no way his dad would ever return, either because he didn't care about his family, or because he was dead. Now, if what Aunt Alice had told him was true, his mother had been working secretly for years to build a time machine that would bring him back. Why hadn't she told him?

And who had taken the machine from his mother's lab? What possible reason would someone have for marooning Professor Zoe Riddle seventy years into the future?

He stopped suddenly, realising where he had seen a diagram that resembled the time machine before. Something very like it had been in the purple folder Mr Blad had been studying in the science staffroom when Cal had interrupted him.

Cal hardly noticed that the Dimbles, accompanied by the O'Hara sisters, were coming his way.

'Yah, Riddle,' said a Dimble, shoving him hard.

Cal's hands curled into fists, but he managed to keep his temper. He'd risk yet another detention if he got involved in a fight, and he couldn't afford to have anything get in the way of finding the time machine.

'Loser!' yelled the other Dimble. The O'Hara sisters smirked.

'Loser, yourself, Dimble.'

'Oh, listen to little Calvin,' sneered Fiona O'Hara, 'standing up for himself.'

Kylie sniffled into a tissue, then announced loudly to no one in particular, 'Have you checked out his aunt? Like, she's weird, just like him.'

There was no point getting into an argument. Cal was already late for the detention and he hated to think what Mr Chortle would say to him when he arrived. Ignoring their jeers, he dodged around the grinning foursome and trotted the last few metres to the gymnasium.

Mr Chortle wasn't waiting in front of the building, as Cal had thought he might be. He wasn't inside, either. Running into a couple of junior students who were collecting a cricket bat and ball for a lunchtime game, Cal said, 'Do you know where Chortle is?'

'In his office,' said one, pushing past Cal.

Mr Chortle's office was tucked in a corner of the gym and was a tiny room, so small that a desk and chair almost completely filled it. Cal checked his watch to find he was nearly six minutes late. Mr Chortle would be furious.

The red door to Mr Chortle's office was half

open. Cal hesitated outside, not looking forward to the angry blast he was sure to receive. He heard Mr Chortle's voice and realised that he was on the phone. Good, maybe he wouldn't notice that Cal wasn't exactly on time.

As he went to knock, Cal heard Mr Chortle say, 'What we don't need is the cops getting involved over a missing person report.'

Cal stopped, his knuckles almost touching the door. Was it possible the conversation was about his mother?

'Who's there?' Mr Chortle had obviously heard him outside the door. 'Come in, whoever you are.'

When Cal opened the door, Mr Chortle said, 'Hold on,' into the phone receiver, then snapped at Cal, 'What do you want?'

'I'm here for detention, sir.'

Mr Chortle made an impatient get-lost gesture with his free hand. 'I haven't got time to bother about detentions now. Later—next week perhaps.' When Cal didn't move fast enough, he added, 'Go on, get out!'

'Yes, sir.'

'And close the door behind you.'

Cal shut the door, but deliberately didn't quite catch the lock. He stood with his hand on the knob and looked around the gym. There was no one else there, and in the silence he could hear Mr Chortle quite clearly.

'We can deal with the situation,' the sports master was saying. 'There's a lot of money involved here, and I want my share, all right?' There was a pause, then Cal heard him say, 'Forget it. I'll make sure the kid knows nothing, so don't worry about it.'

The sound of the receiver being slammed down got Cal moving fast. As silently as possible he ran across the gym and out into the sunlight. He had to find Aunt Alice and tell her what he'd heard.

Aunt Alice, unfortunately, was not easy to find, and it was almost the end of lunchtime when he spotted her chatting to Mr Olnay outside the dining hall. His stomach rumbled loudly, reminding him that he still hadn't eaten.

The most important thing, though, was to tell Aunt Alice about Chortle, so he sidled up to her and Mr Olnay, trying to show by his expression that he had something important to tell her.

The two of them were caught up in a discussion of famous mathematicians, and both ignored him. At last Cal said, 'Aunt Alice?'

'Not now, Cal. Quimby and I are having the most fascinating conversation.'

Quimby? Cal tried not to smile. He'd never known Mr Olnay's first name, and now he knew why. 'Um …' he said.

Aunt Alice and Mr Olnay both glared at him. 'Go away,' said Mr Olnay.

Something reflected the light on the back of Aunt Alice's left hand. With horror Cal saw that she had caught her skin on something and torn it, so that a flap peeled back to reveal the bright metal underneath. So far Mr Olnay hadn't noticed, but that luck couldn't last.

'Aunt Alice? I really need to speak with you.'

'Later. It's not convenient now.' She turned back

to Mr Olnay with a smile. 'You were saying, Quimby?'

Cal gave a yell and collapsed with a thump flat on his back. Mr Olnay and Aunt Alice stopped talking and stared down at him.

'Aunt Alice? Can you help me? I slipped.'

When she leaned over him he grabbed the purple scarf around her neck to keep her head close to him. 'Your hand,' he whispered urgently. 'You've torn your skin.'

She looked at the back of her hand. 'I am feeling consternation,' she said to Cal.

'Is he hurt?' asked Mr Olnay, trying to see over Aunt Alice's shoulder.

'Do something to fix it,' Cal hissed to her.

Aunt Alice straightened up, her right hand casually covering her left. 'There's nothing wrong with you, Cal,' she said. 'So get up and go on your way.'

Cal got up and brushed himself down. 'Sorry,' he said. 'I'm going now.'

He'd talk to Aunt Alice later, but right now he

had just about enough time, before he had to report for monitor duty, to cram something into his mouth and shut his stomach up.

The person sharing monitor duties with Cal turned out to be the sport master's daughter, Tiffany Chortle. When he arrived at the monitors' desk outside the principals' office, she gave him a wide, perfect-toothed smile. 'Hi, Cal.'

'Where's Michele?' said Cal. 'She's supposed to be on with me.'

Cal liked Michele. She was blonde and a bit giggly, and she was smart. Plus she was fun. Tiffany Chortle was blonde too, and she had wide blue eyes, but she was also terribly conceited and used to being the absolute centre of attention.

'Don't ask me,' said Tiffany. 'I suppose someone changed the roster.' She blinked her blue eyes at him. 'Anyway,' she said with a pout, 'I would have thought you'd be pleased it was me.'

'Would you?' said Cal. He had so many ideas and worries spinning in his head that he wasn't particularly interested in making Tiffany feel good.

Tiffany frowned, not at all happy at his response. Fortunately, they were kept occupied running errands for the next few minutes, and when they arrived back at the desk, Ivy Withering had a task for them. The principals had decided that there should be an illustrated history of the school, titled *Withering Mansions Forever*!, and Tiffany and Cal were given the job of sorting into some sort of order a jumble of photographs of events, sports meetings and drama productions that had occurred over the years at Withering Mansions.

Cal was content to sit in silence, going slowly through the photos and putting them into different piles. Tiffany Chortle, quite ignoring a strict school rule, popped a pellet of bubble gum into her mouth. Her jaws moved rhythmically for a while, then she said, 'Is Jen, like, your girlfriend?'

'Oh, *please*.'

Not at all offended by Cal's irritated tone, Tiffany, still chewing, looked at him thoughtfully. 'You spend a lot of time with her.'

'That's because we're friends. I spend a lot of time with Rob and Jen.'

Tiffany chewed on her bubblegum for a moment. 'So, is Jen *Rob's* girlfriend?'

'Why are you asking me?'

Tiffany ducked her head and batted her eyelashes at him. 'Just wondering if you have a girlfriend, that's all.'

This interest from Tiffany Chortle was astonishing, to say the least, and not one bit convincing. Cal said, 'You're telling me you care if I have a girlfriend or not?'

'I might.'

'Yeah, sure.'

Cal busied himself sorting photographs, his expression, he hoped, clearly indicating that he wasn't going to continue with this subject. He hid his suspicion that her interest in him was a set-up, and that Tiffany had been sent by her father to find out what Cal knew. It was unlikely that she was really interested in Cal. Although she might, he suddenly realised, be aiming for Rob, because he was so popular. He grinned to himself. Tiffany wouldn't be at all pleased if she knew what Rob really thought of her.

Tiffany blew another pink bubble, which promptly burst. She used her tongue to collect the gum from her lips and started chewing again. 'Where's your mum?' she said.

'Why are you asking?' said Cal, sounding calm, but on full alert.

Tiffany arranged her face into an expression of deep concern. 'Like, I heard she disappeared. You must be very worried. I know I would be.'

She really was very good-looking, Cal thought. It was hard to imagine that Mr Chortle was her father. Probably Tiffany took after her mother, but whoever she was she'd disappeared long ago. Cal couldn't blame the woman—being married to Mr Chortle would be pretty horrible.

'So,' said Tiffany, not giving up on the subject, 'you know where your mum is, do you?'

'My mother's been called away. Urgent family business.'

'I didn't know you had a family.'

Cal pictured Aunt Alice. 'Oh, I do.'

'You never talk about any of them.'

Cal looked at Tiffany sideways. How would she know whether he had a family or not, anyway? This was the longest conversation she'd ever had with Cal in her life.

'My Aunt Alice has just started teaching at the school,' he said, watching her closely.

Tiffany seemed genuinely puzzled. 'Your aunt? Really?' Her expression changed. 'You don't mean the new English teacher? *She* isn't your aunt, is she?'

'My Aunt Alice,' said Cal, 'is a bit different, but she's very nice.'

Tiffany raised one shoulder in a half-shrug. 'Seems a bit strange she turns up at the school practically the same time your mother disappears, don't you think?'

Cal felt a cold jab of dismay. There was no way Tiffany could know about the time machine and Aunt Alice being an android, could she? 'My mother hasn't disappeared,' he said coldly. He added, thinking it was in a sort of a way true, 'I know exactly where she is.'

'Where?' Tiffany was looking at him with a half-smile, her blue eyes wide, expecting Cal to answer. When he didn't say anything, she leaned closer to him, her smile widening. 'Come on, you can tell me.'

As rudely as he could, Cal said, 'Mind your own business, Tiffany Chortle,' and had the pleasure of seeing her blink with shocked surprise.

'Pssst!'

Cal looked up to see Rob beckoning him from the shelter of a doorway halfway down the corridor. He got up and went to him. 'What's up?'

'Have you heard anything about your mum?'

'No, nothing yet.'

'When Jen and I didn't get to talk to you at lunchtime, we thought one of us should find you and see what's going on.' Rob looked over his shoulder. 'I can't be long—I'm supposed to be getting stuff from the library for Mr Lisher in Geography.'

Cal wished he could tell Rob all about Aunt Alice, but his mother's message had said no one must know. Besides, Tiffany Chortle was leaning in her chair, obviously trying to hear their conversation. 'There's something you can do for me,' he said.

'What?' said Rob. He grinned. 'It isn't anything to do with your aunt, is it?'

Cal dropped his voice to a whisper. 'It's Tiffany,' he said. 'I think Chortle's sent her to spy on me. It's something to do with Mum, but I don't know what.'

Rob looked past him at Tiffany, who, realising she was under observation, sent him a brilliant smile, and called out, 'Hi, Rob.'

'I don't have to be nice to her, do I?' he hissed to Cal.

'If that's what it takes to find out what's going on.' Cal added with a grin, 'I think she likes you.'

Rob gave a disgusted grunt. 'You owe me,' he said.

CHAPTER EIGHT

Mr Chortle had told him to forget the detentions this week, including the one after school, so Cal was free to join most of the students and the two principals on the after-class excursion to Wombat Creek to see a special screening of *Decimator III*. The Witherings had decided that the movie had educational value, although Cal thought the real reason was that both the Witherings were big fans of the action star, Baxter Swithenbottom.

Under normal circumstances, Cal would have

been first on the bus, as he had really enjoyed *Decimator I* and *II*, but these were not in any way normal circumstances. Ignoring catcalls from the Dimbles, Cal waved to Jen and Rob as the first of the two chartered buses began to chug off from the front of the school. Tiffany Chortle, who seemed determined to ignore the fact that Cal hadn't been very friendly to her, waved to him from the bus.

He saw Jen look at Tiffany, and then at Cal. Jen pointed to Tiffany, then put her fingers in her mouth and pretended she was vomiting, which made Cal laugh. It didn't feel right letting Rob and Jen think he still had a detention with Chortle. But there was no way he could tell them the truth, because they'd want to join in, and he had to do this alone.

He guessed that Aunt Alice was spending the afternoon using her detective arts to look for clues, and now, with most of the school out of the way, Cal intended to do a little detective work of his own. Five minutes ago he'd seen Aunt Alice in conversation with Morris Blad outside the library, so this was a good time to find the purple folder

Mr Blad had so quickly closed when Cal had knocked at the door.

Acting casual, Cal put his hands in his pockets and strolled in the direction of the science department. He'd only gone a short way when the Witherings, rushing to join the second bus, came into view. Cal tried to dodge them, but it was too late.

'You're not going to see *Decimator III*?' said Alistair Withering, his tone indicating that he could hardly believe anyone would willingly miss such a treat.

Cal drooped his shoulders and tried to look as depressed as possible. 'I don't feel like it,' he mumbled.

'Of course you don't,' yelled Ivy Withering, clapping Cal on the shoulder so hard that he staggered. 'Really, Alistair, you can be so insensitive. The boy has a lot of things on his mind. That's right, isn't it Cal?'

'Um … well, yes.'

The driver of the bus gave a blast on his horn,

causing Alistair Withering to leap from foot to foot. 'We can't miss the bus! Hurry!'

Cal watched the Witherings scramble onto the bus to cheers from the students and teachers already seated, then the bus chugged off down the driveway.

He was almost to the science department building when he heard raised voices and saw Mr Chortle in a scarlet and blue tracksuit approaching with Mr Sykes. Cal ducked behind a handy clump of bushes, and peered at them through the branches.

When Mr Sykes was with his wife, Big Bertha from the school office, he looked insignificant and hardly opened his mouth. He wasn't acting that way with Mr Chortle, though. In fact, Mr Sykes was very obviously furious, and seemed to be telling Mr Chortle exactly what he thought.

With his large, pitted nose jutting over his droopy grey moustache, he looked a bit like a strange, angry bird. As Cal watched, Mr Sykes took something out of the pocket of his khaki overalls and waved it at Mr Chortle. Mr Chortle made an attempt to snatch it, but Mr Sykes ripped whatever it was away before he could get his fingers on it.

As they came closer, Cal could hear Mr Sykes was saying, '… and I don't like this mystery stuff at all.' He gestured with the thing he'd taken from his pocket. Squinting, Cal could make out that it was a flat, rectangular piece of plastic that flashed when it caught the light.

'As far as I'm concerned,' Mr Sykes went on, 'it's a piece of expensive scientific equipment, so I'm taking it to the Witherings.'

'I've told you, Sykes. It's mine. Now give it to me,' Mr Chortle demanded, his face blotchy with rage. 'It's my private property, so you can't just hand it over to someone else.'

Mr Sykes stopped walking and so did Mr Chortle. Swinging around to face the sports master, he said, 'If it's yours, what is it? You couldn't tell me when I asked you. And what was it doing in the middle of my compost heap? You tell me that!'

Mr Chortle's balding head was almost as red as his face. 'I don't know what it was doing in your blasted compost heap, Sykes, but I want it back right now.'

'No way,' said Mr Sykes. 'It looks like something valuable, so I'll give it to the Witherings, and they can decide what to do with it.'

'The Witherings aren't in the school at the moment,' snapped Mr Chortle.

'Fine! Then I'll keep it until they are.'

After a final angry glance at Mr Chortle, Mr Sykes turned around and marched back the way they had just come. The sports master stood staring after him, then, swearing to himself, he hurried toward the teachers' accommodation.

Cal waited until he was sure both of them had disappeared before he came out of the shelter of the bushes. He shivered. The late afternoon sun had no heat in it and a cold wind was sweeping across the green fields surrounding the school. Cal was glad to reach the shelter of the science building.

There was no one around except the cleaner, Mr

Jenkins, a thin man in overalls too big for him, who was trundling along the corridor emptying rubbish bins from each classroom into a large wheeled bin. Remembering that he'd read somewhere that as long as you looked as though you knew exactly what you were doing and where you were going, no one would challenge you, Cal walked confidently toward the science staffroom.

'Where you going, boy?' challenged the cleaner when Cal drew level with him.

Cal stopped. 'Going, Mr Jenkins?' he said vaguely.

'This area's off-limits to students after school. That is, unless you've got a good reason to be here.' He waited, his narrow head cocked expectantly, for Cal to answer.

Cal said, 'I'm here to see Mr Blad.'

'He's not here,' said the cleaner, looking pleased to be giving what he obviously believed was disappointing information. 'He's gone. In fact, all of the teachers have gone for the day.'

'Mr Blad told me to wait for him in the science staffroom,' Cal lied. 'I'm sure he'll be back.'

Mr Jenkins shrugged as he turned back to his work. 'Suit yourself, then.'

The science staffroom seemed even more untidy than it had been that morning. As the cleaner had said, the place was empty, but even so Cal tiptoed in, feeling as if any moment someone would pop up from behind the furniture and demand to know what he was doing there.

Mr Blad's desk appeared to have had yet another layer of books and papers added to those already deposited there this morning. The purple folder wasn't anywhere obvious, and Cal didn't expect that it would be. Of course, Mr Blad could have locked it away in a drawer, or taken it with him when he left.

None of the three drawers in the desk was locked, and each was filled with papers and other bits and pieces. In the top drawer Cal found a shrivelled apple and a cheese sandwich so old that it looked like a fossil.

Cal stood back and tried to imagine where he would hide a purple folder so it wouldn't be found. He looked around. Next to Mr Blad's desk was a tall, battered bookcase crammed with books leaning in all directions, loose sheets of paper, ring folders, various pieces of scientific equipment and several rock samples. The second top shelf, however, was much tidier than the others. Here there were only textbooks, all set neatly in a row, their spines upright.

The shelf was too high to reach easily, so Cal climbed onto Mr Blad's chair. The folder was there, shoved down behind the row of books!

Balancing on the chair, Cal opened the folder. It contained several diagrams that were a little like his mother's time machine, each surrounded with a bewildering pattern of formulae and written comments.

The one he was looking for was the last of the diagrams. Cal studied it carefully until he was sure that it was identical to the diagram in the message from his mother Aunt Alice had given him.

There was one difference: with a shock of angry surprise Cal realised that the words underneath the diagram had been altered. Now they read, THE BLAD TEMPORAL SHIFTER.

CHAPTER NINE

Cal had just got down from the chair when his heart lurched at the sound of voices in the corridor. He heard Mr Jenkins say, 'Has someone in the science department changed the lock on my storage room? I can't get into it.'

There was a murmured answer, then the cleaner said loudly, 'Well, I'm not cleaning this department until I can get to my equipment, that's all I can say.'

There was a rumble of his wheeled bin as he

moved away, followed by the tap, tap, tap of high heels coming Cal's way. He checked out the shelf to make sure the purple folder he'd put back was completely out of sight, then he swept a pile of exercise books off a rickety wooden chair and quickly sat down.

Ms Hufflet stopped at the sight of him. 'Well, well, well,' she said, 'if it isn't Calvin Riddle. May I ask what you're doing here after class?'

It was probably wise to stick to the same story he'd told before, so Cal said, 'I'm waiting for Mr Blad.'

'Waiting for Morris Blad?' She tossed back her long black hair with a scornful laugh. 'Then you'll be waiting for some time. He always leaves the moment the last bell of the day sounds.'

Cal stood up. 'I'll be going, then.'

'Not so fast.' Her sharp features were full of curiosity. 'Exactly what are you seeing Mr Blad about?'

Ms Hufflet had been trying to get into his mother's lab that morning, so maybe she knew something. Cal said, 'I was going to ask Mr Blad about my mum. She's been called away and I'm not sure where she is. I thought Mr Blad might have some ideas.' He put on what he hoped was a pathetic expression. 'I don't suppose you'd know anything, do you?'

Ms Hufflet frowned, then her face went soft with sympathy. 'I'm sorry, Calvin, I can't help you. I've been looking everywhere for Zoe myself.'

She dumped books off another battered chair and pulled it closer to sit beside him. 'Perhaps I shouldn't tell you this, but something peculiar has been going on lately, and Morris Blad seems to be in the middle of it. I've heard your mother's name mentioned in whispered telephone conversations, and Frank Chortle, who's never been in the habit of having anything to do with the science department, has taken to dropping in regularly.'

'Mr Chortle doesn't like Mum.'

'No, he doesn't, but that's because of something that happened long ago before I came to Withering Mansions. I've been told Mr Chortle was very keen on your mother, and after your father left, he kept asking her out, but Zoe refused every time. He's never forgiven her for turning him down.'

Deciding to take a chance on being direct, Cal said, 'I saw you trying to get into Mum's room this morning.'

Ms Hufflet arched her eyebrows. 'Did you? I'd decided to talk to Zoe about what was going on, but I couldn't find her. Her little lab was the last place I checked.'

Cal wasn't sure he believed Noreen Hufflet. She sounded sincere and she was looking at him with a kind, sympathetic expression, but this could just be a trick to get him to tell her what he knew.

With a particularly warm smile, she said, 'Calvin, I wonder if you could help me with something. You may not know this, but *I* was the teacher mentioned at the assembly. It was from my purse that things were stolen.'

'Really?' said Cal.

'And I wonder if you've heard anything. Perhaps

some of the other students have been talking about it.' She leaned closer. 'Perhaps you know who the culprit is.'

'What did they take?'

Ms Hufflet leaned back in her chair. 'Money, of course. And a few odds and ends. Nothing very valuable, but I'd like them back.'

'I'm sorry, I haven't heard anything.' He stood up. 'I'd better go.'

'Your aunt is staying with you, isn't she?'

'Aunt Alice. Have you met her?'

'She introduced herself to me this afternoon,' said Ms Hufflet with an odd expression on her face. 'We had an interesting conversation about the weather.'

With dismay Cal recalled that he had suggested to Aunt Alice that she should discuss a safe topic like the weather when meeting people for the first time. 'My aunt's interested in things like the weather,' he remarked.

'She certainly is,' said Ms Hufflet. 'I must say that I don't believe I've met an English teacher before who knew quite so much about global weather systems. And she seemed to be an expert on air quality, ocean currents and the effect of high altitude jet streams.'

'That's my Aunt Alice,' said Cal with an effort at stopping himself from rolling his eyes. Heaven knows what she'd said to other teachers!

When he left the staffroom he found Einstein waiting for him. At least, the cat *seemed* to be waiting for him. As soon as Cal appeared Einstein stood up, and, looking back over his ginger shoulder, walked a few steps down the corridor, then stopped and miaowed.

'What's the matter? Are you hungry?' As the official Withering Mansions cat Einstein was fed at the dining hall kitchens every day. But he also managed to scrounge treats from several people around the school, including Cal's mother, with whom he spent a lot of time.

Einstein twitched his whiskers, walked on another few steps and miaowed again. It was obvious he expected Cal to follow him, so Cal did.

Round the corner they went, Cal following the upright ginger tail.

Einstein halted in front of a padlocked door with a sign that read STORAGE, and gave Cal a meaningful look.

'What are you showing me this for?'

Einstein sighed.

Cal jiggled the large, shiny and new padlock. It was locked tight. 'You're saying something is in here I should see?'

A twitch of ginger whiskers.

'I wish you could talk.'

The cat blinked.

'Cal?' Ms Hufflet's voice came from around the corner. 'Is that you? Are you still here?'

Cal and Einstein looked at each other, then Cal ran on tiptoes for the exit while Einstein turned and strolled sedately toward the staffroom.

'Ms Hufflet says you talked to her about the weather,' said Cal to Aunt Alice when he found her back at the apartment.

A note of pride in her voice, Aunt Alice said, 'I also chatted to Quimby Olnay about mathematics, Bertha Sykes about abnormal psychology—'

'Abnormal psychology?'

'Yes, she mentioned something about someone being mad, and I took the opportunity to discuss the more interesting forms of insanity.'

'Oh, great!'

Ignoring his comment, she went on, 'And I chatted with Morris Blad about dinosaurs. He was very interested to hear about the latest discoveries.'

'Aunt Alice! You didn't talk about the future fossil finds, did you?'

She shot out her bottom lip in a pout. 'I may have, but I'm sure he didn't notice. And I chatted to Frank Chortle about the weather, although he didn't show much interest in global warming, and I made several jokes, but Frank didn't laugh. No sense of humour, I suppose. And then I chatted with Burt Sykes about maggots and grubs—'

She broke off to send Cal a defiant look. 'Not my idea. Burt insisted on bringing up the subject of his compost heap and mulching activities and the role of various creatures in decomposition …'

As Aunt Alice went on, listing the people she'd spoken with, Cal realised with amazement that she had managed to talk to almost every adult at Withering Mansions School.

'… but my favourite chat,' Aunt Alice said, 'was with Noreen Hufflet. She's very charming, and extremely interested in the ultimate fate of the ozone layer.'

'I saw her trying to get into Mum's lab this morning.'

Aunt Alice, who was seated on the pea-green couch—and clashing horribly with it—was closely inspecting the television remote. She turned her head sharply. 'Is that so? Noreen Hufflet is not one of my suspects.' She held out the remote to Cal. 'This is very primitive technology.'

'Who are your suspects?'

'Well …' Aunt Alice wriggled her shoulders uncomfortably. 'I am abashed,' she said.

'What?'

'I lack a list of suspects. I have not, as yet, discovered anything useful. I am feeling an emotion—humiliation, I believe it is.'

Cal knew what *he* was feeling: pleased with himself. 'I have a list of possible suspects.'

Aunt Alice's nose twitched. 'Indeed?' she said.

'There's Mr Chortle, Mr Sykes, Mr Blad and Ms Hufflet. And I'm not absolutely sure about the Witherings.'

'Your mother assured me the Witherings are to be trusted.'

'Maybe she's wrong.'

Aunt Alice's eyebrows flew up until they almost disappeared into her red wig. 'Professor Zoe Riddle wrong? I would assess that at being most unlikely.'

'Someone's got the time machine,' said Cal reasonably. 'It could be the Witherings.'

With a metallic creak of her knees, Aunt Alice abruptly stood to attention. 'My task is to find the device. Tell me everything you have observed today. Leave out no detail, however small. My detective arts are designed to deal with the tiniest clue.'

'I think I know where—'

'You must start at the beginning. That is the logical thing to do.'

'But—'

Aunt Alice was stern. 'From the moment you got up this morning, please, in chronological order.'

Starting with the shock of waking up late for gym, Cal went through his whole day, including the argument he'd overheard between Mr Chortle and Mr Sykes.

Aunt Alice was particularly interested in the plastic rectangle that Sykes had refused to give to Chortle. 'Describe it exactly.'

When he had finished, she clapped her hands together. 'That sounds very much like a whuffling switcher, a vital component of the time machine! Where is it at this moment?'

'Mr Sykes has it, but he won't give it to you. He told Mr Chortle that he would wait and hand it over to the Witherings when they got back.'

'The Witherings will let me have it,' said Aunt Alice cheerfully. Her face fell. 'Of course, we are still no closer to finding the time machine itself.'

Cal said, 'I think I might know where it is.'

Aunt Alice's mouth dropped open. 'I am feeling astonishment,' she announced. 'Indeed, I am shocked. My detective arts have not located it, so how can it be that you have been able to do this?'

'Einstein showed me.'

'Really?' said Aunt Alice. 'I understand that you are making a joke, because I have a sense of humour. I am not laughing, however. The famous genius, Albert Einstein, is no longer alive, so he could not possibly have shown you anything.'

'This is another Einstein. He's a ginger cat.' Cal explained how he'd been led to the padlocked storage room, and that earlier he'd heard the cleaner complaining about how the lock had been changed.

An expression of deep doubt filled Aunt Alice's face. 'A feline indicated this?' she said. 'Their species is not noted for being helpful.'

'I'm sure he was trying to tell me that the time machine is locked inside that storage room.'

'Very well,' said Aunt Alice. 'Tonight, when everyone is asleep, we must find out.'

CHAPTER TEN

People who had gone on the trip to see *Decimator III* were to have a late meal in the dining hall—that is, if they hadn't already stuffed themselves with McDonald's hamburgers at Wombat Creek.

It was decided that Cal would go to the hall to see what Rob had found out from Tiffany Chortle, and Aunt Alice would find the Witherings to find out if Mr Sykes had handed over the whuffling switcher and if so, ask them to give it to her. Then Aunt Alice would join the staff in their separate dining area and observe Mr Chortle, Mr Blad and Ms Hufflet if they were there. If not, she was to strike up conversations with the other teachers to see if she could gain any useful information.

'I have jokes,' said Aunt Alice, 'so I will entertain them all.' She shot her eyebrows up and down, and asked Cal, 'What is pink and blue and white all over?'

Seeing that she was waiting expectantly for him to respond, Cal said with a sigh, 'I don't know. What *is* pink and blue and white all over?'

'A gudfrank!' said Aunt Alice, triumphant. 'Ha, ha!' she added.

'What's a gudfrank?'

Aunt Alice looked confused, then flustered. 'Oh,' she said, 'the gudfrank isn't invented yet. Sorry.'

'Is this the kind of joke you've been telling people?'

She wriggled her shoulders. 'Maybe.'

Cal groaned. 'No more jokes. This is too important.'

Aunt Alice was rather sulky at this and complained that she had very little opportunity to use her sense of humour programming, but Cal made her promise to be serious.

The dining hall was full of chattering students, all discussing *Decimator III*. 'It was great,' said Rob when Cal joined him in the line for food.

Cal interrupted him before he could get going about the movie. 'What about Tiffany?'

'Tiffany!' said Rob, rolling his eyes dramatically. 'Well?'

His friend looked smug. 'She told me all about it. It was easy. I just smiled at her and she talked her head off.'

Cal was impatient. 'Look, I haven't got time to waste. Are you going to tell me or not?'

'Okay, but I'd like to know what's going on.'

'I'll tell you later.'

Rob made a face at him, but went on, 'Tiffany said her father changed the roster so she'd be on monitor duty with you. He told her to see if you had any idea where your mother was, and what she'd been working on lately. Chortle particularly asked her to find out whatever she could about your aunt. Then there was something about diagrams in a purple folder. I don't know what that was about, and neither did Tiffany.'

'That's it?'

Rob looked indignant. 'That's a lot! You didn't have to be nice to Tiffany Chortle, like I did!'

At the serving counter at the head of the line, Kylie O'Hara's voice rose above the hum of conversation. 'It's not fair! You gave her more mashed potato than me!'

The woman behind the counter told Kylie to move along and stop holding up the line.

'I'm not moving until I get more potato. And gravy.'

Someone tapped Cal on the shoulder. He turned around to see that it was Jim Taylor, who'd been on monitor duty with Kylie that morning.

Jim's face was twisted with dislike. 'I'd love to dob Kylie in,' he said. 'I'm sure she's the one who stole the things from Ms Hufflet's desk.'

'How come?'

'You know that *Trumpheter* she had? Well, Hufflet confiscated it the day before, and I heard Kylie telling her sister that she'd get the magazine back, no matter what, and that Hufflet would be sorry she'd taken it in the first place.'

'That doesn't prove anything,' said Rob.

Cal thought it was a very likely that Kylie had stolen something from Hufflet. What if Ms Hufflet had the whuffling switcher hidden in her purse, and Kylie, thinking it might be worth something, had taken it?

He had already decided that Mr Chortle and Mr Blad were working together to steal the time machine, but what if Ms Hufflet was involved too? What if it was Chortle and Ms Hufflet who were responsible for the theft? If so, what was Mr Blad doing with the purple folder and the diagram he had changed to read the Blad Temporal Shifter?

The line had shuffled along and they were up to

the serving counter. Cal collected a tray, took a plate loaded with mashed potato, gravy and chicken, and looked around to see where Kylie O'Hara was sitting. 'See you later,' he said to Rob.

'Where are you going?'

'To sit with Kylie,' said Cal, laughing at Rob's expression.

Naturally Kylie was blowing her nose when he arrived at the table where she was sitting with her poisonous sister. 'What do you want?' snapped Fiona when he slid his tray onto their table. 'Get lost, Riddle.'

Cal ignored her. He sat on a spare chair and said to Kylie, 'You were the one who stole the things from Ms Hufflet.'

'I was not!' Her pink nose quivered and she dabbed at it with yet another tissue.

Gambling that he was right, Cal said, 'When the science staffroom was empty, you sneaked in to get your stupid magazine, and while you were there you went through her purse and took money and a flat, plastic rectangle.'

Kylie glared at him, but she looked worried. Cal went on, 'When the assembly was called, and all that fuss was made, you got scared, so you got rid of the plastic thing.'

'That's a lie!'

'Actually,' said Cal, 'you threw it on Mr Sykes's compost heap.'

Kylie's expression of astonishment was enough proof for Cal. Without another word he stood, picked up his tray and walked away, leaving the two sisters staring after him.

'Attention! Attention everyone!' yelled a voice from the front of the dining hall.

It was Ivy Withering. When the buzz of conversation died down, she bellowed, 'Until further notice, no one is to enter the science building. Mr Blad has detected a serious gas leak that could lead to an explosion, so the building is closed. Repairs will be done tomorrow as soon as we can get someone from Wombat Creek. In the meantime, a list of alternative classrooms will be posted in the quad.'

Cal put his tray down on the nearest table. He wasn't hungry any more. He had to find Aunt Alice. Before he could start looking, she appeared at the doorway and made her way over the hall to him, as usual causing heads to turn.

'The Witherings had the whuffling shifter,' she said in a loud whisper when she reached him. She patted the pocket of her lime-green skirt. 'Now I have it.'

Taking care to check that no one was listening, Cal said in a low voice, 'We can't get into the science building tonight. There's supposed to be a gas leak.'

'Let us investigate.' Aunt Alice strode off and Cal hurried to keep up with her. As he went past the Dimbles, who had double helpings of everything heaped on their plates, one of the twins put out his foot to trip Cal.

Cal stumbled, and the Dimbles jeered. Aunt Alice looked around. She fixed the Dimbles with her black eyes and their loud voices faded away.

'Those boys will be in my English class

tomorrow,' said Aunt Alice when Cal caught up with her. 'I look forward to it.'

Outside it was dark and very cold. Diamond stars twinkled overhead, and a stiff breeze blew into their faces. The science building had been illuminated with floodlights, and hastily painted cardboard signs reading DANGER! DO NOT ENTER were set up at intervals. Cal and his aunt circled the entire building and found a member of the school office staff, each one wearing layers of warm clothing, on guard duty at every entrance.

Aunt Alice pursed her lips into the odd O-shape that made Cal want to laugh. 'Our plans may need to change. At least no one can take the time machine from the building.'

Catching sight of Mr Blad, who was standing at the edge of the circle of lights, one hand rammed in his jacket pocket, the other pulling at his new beard, Cal said to Aunt Alice, 'There's Mr Blad. I think he's made up the story about the gas leak.'

'I am feeling determined and purposeful,' declared Aunt Alice. 'Let us question Morris Blad.

He and I had a very pleasant conversation this afternoon.'

Mr Blad saw them coming and quickly began walking away. Aunt Alice accelerated and grabbed him by the arm. 'Morris,' she said, 'we wish to question you.'

Trying to pull away from her, he muttered, 'Let me go. I have to see someone.'

'Did you steal the diagram from my mother?' said Cal.

Mr Blad struggled to free his arm from Aunt Alice's grip, but she held him without apparent effort. He said, 'Cal, I don't know what you're talking about.'

'I'm talking about the Blad Temporal Shifter. At least that's what you've changed it to read.'

Aunt Alice shook Mr Blad. To Cal it seemed she didn't use much effort, but she nearly lifted the teacher off his feet. 'Answer the boy.'

All the fight went out of Blad. Aunt Alice released him and he rubbed his arm as he said, 'All right, I'll tell you. I found the diagram in Noreen's desk. I knew she had something hidden there. I'd heard about Zoe's attempts to build a time machine and how close she was to success, so I recognised exactly what it was when I found it.'

'Why did you take Mum's name off?' demanded Cal. 'It's her machine, not yours.'

Mr Blad hung his head. 'It's been my dream for years to construct a time machine, but I've never succeeded. For weeks I've been listening to Frank Chortle and Noreen whispering together about something big that was going to make them a lot of money, and I knew it must be your mother's temporal shifter. When she didn't turn up this morning, I borrowed Burt Sykes's security master key, but it didn't fit your mother's electronic lock. So I used the master key to get into your apartment and search for the lab keycard there, but I didn't find it. You almost caught me when you came home.'

'Do you know where the time machine is?' Aunt Alice took a step closer to him and Blad shrank back. 'We need the location.'

'I'm sure it's somewhere in the science building.

I knew Frank and Noreen would probably try to move it tonight, so I made up the story about the gas leak, thinking that would stop them, and I'd have a chance to search and find the machine after everyone had gone to bed. But the Witherings have posted guards on the building, so I can't get in.'

'The authorities must be notified,' said Aunt Alice.

Mr Blad stared at her. 'Authorities? Do you mean the police?'

'Yes. Law enforcement. You have committed a crime.'

Mr Blad's face crumpled. 'Oh, no, please. I'll be ruined!'

Aunt Alice put her hands on his shoulders and he winced. She said, slowly and with great emphasis, 'We could let you go. But you must say nothing to anyone. Not one person. If you do …'

'I won't! I won't! I promise.'

Mr Blad looked hopefully at Aunt Alice. She removed her hands and said, 'You have one chance.'

Watching Blad scuttle off into the darkness, Cal said, 'Wow.'

'Yes,' said Aunt Alice, smiling proudly. 'That was wow.'

'What do we do now?'

'I have a plan,' said Aunt Alice.

Cal looked at her doubtfully. 'You do?'

'We will go to the Witherings tonight and discuss how we will set a trap for tomorrow, after the building is inspected, and it is opened up again.'

CHAPTER ELEVEN

'Good morning!' exclaimed Aunt Alice, striding into the classroom for the first lesson of the day. 'Are we all ready for an invigorating English lesson?'

The students who'd been chattering stopped for a moment, then the noise began again. Cal, sitting in the front row between Jen and Rob, watched Aunt Alice's face change from enthusiasm to extreme irritation.

He checked her over quickly, in case something

was wrong since he had last seen her. At least she had her hair on straight, but the long red and green tartan socks she was wearing with her black ankle boots clashed terribly with her glaring orange skirt and purple-and-pink striped blouse. And, of course, everything clashed with her hair.

'Attention, class!' Aunt Alice swept the room with her dark, laser-like glance, and silence followed wherever she looked.

'Jeez!' said someone in the hush. 'Get her, willya!'

The speaker was, Cal saw with pleasure, a Dimble. George and Bruce were sitting at the very back of the class, tilting their chairs— entirely against Withering Mansions rules— against the wall.

'George Dimble,' said Aunt Alice with a cold smile, 'come to the front of the room.'

Smirking, one of the Dimbles dropped his chair onto its four legs and stood up.

'No,' said Aunt Alice. 'I want George. You are Bruce.'

Both the Dimbles, and indeed, the rest of the class, looked surprised. No one could reliably tell the Dimble twins apart. The other Dimble slammed his chair down onto all its legs and got to his feet. 'Yeah?' he said, folding his fat arms in front of his chest. 'Whatcha want?'

Someone giggled and George Dimble looked around, grinning triumphantly. The Dimbles usually caused trouble in their classes and very few teachers could handle them. Cal's mother was one of the successful teachers, but even she had difficulty with the Dimbles at times.

'Look at me, George Dimble,' said Aunt Alice.

George sniggered. 'That's pretty hard to do.' His smile faded as his eyes locked on Aunt Alice's. 'Ah …' he said.

'Come here, George Dimble.' She pointed to a spot beside her. 'You are volunteering to demonstrate Koga to the class.'

'Don't do it, George,' said Bruce Dimble, who had again tilted his chair. 'Tell her to get lost.'

George didn't seem to hear his brother. Along

with the rest of the students, Cal watched fascinated as George obediently walked to the front of the class and stood, arms hanging at his sides, at the place indicated.

'It's like he's hypnotised or something,' whispered Jen to Cal.

'What's Koga?' said Rob. 'I've never heard of it.'

Cal remembered Aunt Alice had said that Koga was something special she'd been programmed to teach. 'I'm not sure, but I think it's going to be good.'

'Your attention, students,' said Aunt Alice. 'Koga is a system of bodily positions, combined with verbal sounds. It has been shown to enhance mental processes. Koga will be discovered by the famous Dr Eugenie Blatfors in the year—'

She broke off as she caught sight of Cal frantically waving at her. Aunt Alice frowned at him, then went slightly pink. 'I mean, of course, that Koga *was* discovered by Dr Eugenie Blatfors, who is not yet famous. But she will be.'

'What do you do?' asked Jen.

'I will use George Dimble to demonstrate,' said Aunt Alice. 'Everyone, watch very closely.'

She crooked a finger at George, who stepped closer. Turning to the class, she said, 'The first position is designed to aid all mathematical calculations. It is called the Pose of the Computational Heron. When this position is done correctly, the subject will find that problems which previously were difficult are now much easier to solve.'

There was a muffled snigger from the back of the room.

'Is mathematics your best subject, Bruce Dimble?' asked Aunt Alice.

'Not likely.'

'Then I suggest you pay close attention to your brother's demonstration, as you obviously need help in the mathematics area. George, follow my instructions.'

In a few moments George, without one murmur of complaint, was twisted into an extraordinary position. He was standing on his left leg with his knee bent, his right leg extended straight out behind him, toe pointed. His head was tucked under his left arm, and his other arm was swinging in wide circles. At the top of each revolution he shouted, 'Yip! Yip! Yip!'

A breeze of laughter flowed through the room, and Cal couldn't resist smiling. It was so good to see a bully like George Dimble making a fool of himself.

Bruce Dimble, his face flushed with fury, stalked to the front of the class. 'Look, you freak,' he said, pushing his face close to Aunt Alice's, 'no one does this to a Dimble.'

'Bruce, you can help,' said Aunt Alice, staring deep into his eyes. 'I need someone to demonstrate the Pose of the Musical Gnat to the class.'

In no time at all, Bruce Dimble was chest-down on the floor, his legs extended behind him and arms held out from his body and flapping strongly like fat wings. He held his chin high and was singing, 'Buzz-a-biddy, buzz-a-biddy,' over and over, up and down the scale.

Rob said to Cal. 'Can your aunt make all of us do that? By hypnotising us?'

'It is not hypnotism,' said Aunt Alice, over-hearing Rob. 'It is linking with deep brainwaves. And this can only be done with a very small number of humans who have certain personalities—usually bullies who have not developed their mental skills.'

A little boy on monitor duty knocked at the door, came in and handed Aunt Alice a note. She read it quickly, then motioned to Cal. 'It's time,' she said to him. 'The inspection of the science building is almost complete.'

Turning to George and Bruce, she said, 'Thank you for your assistance in the Koga demonstration.' The Dimbles, looking dazed and rather puzzled, went back to their seats without a word.

As the bell went for the end of the lesson, Aunt Alice said, 'Students, you are to practise these two Koga poses in your own time. If you have trouble, I'm sure George and Bruce Dimble will be pleased to assist you.'

A A A

The science building had been declared completely safe but classes had not yet resumed, so the corridors and laboratories were still empty.

Einstein sat outside the cleaner's storage room, washing his face and whiskers. He had just begun to clean behind his ginger ears when Ms Hufflet and Mr Chortle came hurrying along the corridor.

'Blasted cat!' exclaimed Mr Chortle, aiming a kick at him. Einstein jumped out of the way, hissing, his fur puffed up with rage. He crouched down, out of reach, his tail lashing wildly.

Ms Hufflet grabbed the sport master's arm. 'Don't waste time, Frank. We only have a few minutes.'

Mr Chortle fiddled with the padlock, swearing, until it opened. He flung wide the storage room door. 'Come on, Noreen. We have to get the time machine out of the building fast and into the back of my van. Then we have to get the whuffling shifter from the Witherings.'

Nestled in the mops, brushes, buckets and tins of

cleaning supplies was an object covered by a grubby sheet. They wrestled it out of the storage room, Mr Chortle saying, 'Careful, careful. Don't drop it.'

When they got it out into the hall they put it down, and Mr Chortle whipped the sheet off. 'There,' he said. 'Isn't it beautiful? And it's going to make us a lot of money.'

Cal stepped out of the doorway of the next room, where he'd been hiding. 'That's my mother's time machine,' he said.

Ms Hufflet was the first to recover. 'No, you're mistaken, Calvin,' she said, managing a strained smile. 'Now, what are you doing out of class?'

Beside her, Mr Chortle looked as if he was going to explode. 'Come here, boy,' he commanded.

Keeping his distance, Cal said, 'The machine is called the Riddle Temporal Shifter. It's called that because it's named after my mother. She invented it. When she used it to go into the future, you fixed the machine so she couldn't come back.'

'We'll have to take the boy with us,' said Mr Chortle to Ms Hufflet, 'and deal with him later.'

Ms Hufflet looked rather sick. 'Frank, that's kidnapping. I don't—'

'After we've gone this far, I'm not giving up now.' He made a sudden lunge at Cal, managing to grab the front of his shirt.

With a low growl Einstein made a graceful leap, landing on Mr Chortle's shoulders, and sinking his claws in deeply. Mr Chortle yelled, let go of Cal and twisted around, trying to get a grip on Einstein, who was now yowling triumphantly, every ginger hair on end.

'Now what's this then?' said a deep voice.

Ms Hufflet gasped. Einstein jumped down. Mr Chortle stared at the two police officers who had stepped out of the same room Cal had been in.

'Nothing's happening, officer,' said Mr Chortle to the one who had spoken. He gave a weak smile. 'Just some trouble with a cat and—'

He broke off as Aunt Alice and the Witherings appeared from the room.

The officer said, 'We heard everything, sir. I'm afraid you and Ms Hufflet are under arrest.'

Einstein sat down and began to wash one paw. Cal could hear him purring. He looked up at Cal and blinked his yellow eyes. Cal could swear that the cat was smiling.

CHAPTER TWELVE

Aunt Alice was on her knees, fiddling with the innards of the time machine. Her orange skirt had a smear of black on it, and her long red-and-green tartan socks had fallen down to wrinkle around her ankles.

'There,' she said, sitting back. 'The whuffling shifter is in place. I have made the other necessary repairs. The machine should work faultlessly now.'

The Witherings had gone off with the police and the two teachers, leaving Cal and Aunt Alice to carefully carry the time machine back to his mother's lab and put it in the corner where it belonged.

The last thing Cal heard from Mr Chortle and Ms Hufflet, as they were marched off in handcuffs, was Mr Chortle insisting he was innocent and that it was all Ms Hufflet's idea, and Ms Hufflet saying *she* was innocent and it was Mr Chortle alone who had masterminded the whole scheme.

The time machine began a gentle hum and the three green loops of tubing grew brighter in colour. 'It's warming up,' said Aunt Alice.

'What happens now?'

'I have made adjustments, and I should arrive exactly seventy years into the future.'

Aunt Alice sat herself down on the translucent chair, pulled up her tartan socks, and then punched several keys on the control panel set into the arm of the chair. The humming increased, the green tubing became brighter still, and she disappeared.

Cal felt a sudden sense of loss. He probably

would never see Aunt Alice again. He knew, of course, she wasn't really his aunt, but he felt that somehow she was a relative of his, and no matter how much trouble she'd caused he would miss her an awful lot.

The time machine sat quietly in the corner, its humming very faint. Cal couldn't look anywhere else. His heart beat fast with excitement. Any moment now, he hoped, his mother would materialise.

Nothing happened for what seem ages and Cal was beginning to have the sick feeling that the machine wasn't repaired after all, when it began to hum more loudly and the green tubing glowed brightly.

'Cal!'

His mother sat there, smiling the widest smile he had ever seen on her face. She looked just the same as usual, a bit tired perhaps.

They hugged for a long time. 'Why didn't you tell me about the time machine?' he said at last.

'I'm sorry, darling. I didn't want to get your

hopes up, when it was so likely I wouldn't succeed. As it is, I haven't been able to find your father, but I have hopes that I will very soon be able to locate him. I suppose the android told you all about it.'

'Don't call her an android, Mum. She's more than that. She's Aunt Alice.'

His mother ruffled his hair. 'She is quite a character. She gave me a full report as soon as she appeared.' Her face became grim. 'I wasn't surprised to hear that Frank Chortle was involved, but I never would have believed that Noreen Hufflet would do such a thing.'

'It was Aunt Alice's plan to trap them.'

His mother hugged him again. 'I'm glad she was a help to you.'

'I'm going to miss her.'

The time machine, which had been sitting almost silently, suddenly woke up and began to hum. As they looked at it in surprise, Aunt Alice suddenly appeared.

'I'm back!' she announced.

'Aren't you required in the future?' said Cal's

mother. 'I understood that I was only borrowing your services for as long as was needed.'

'Well, I do have to go back eventually,' said Aunt Alice, getting up and straightening her purple-and-pink striped blouse, 'but I'll do that some other time.'

She looked at them expectantly. 'It is my sense of humour. You get it? Some other time? I can time travel some other time.' She beamed at them. 'You see the joke? Some other time?'

'Hey, not bad,' said Cal.

Aunt Alice clasped her hands together with delight. 'I am feeling funny,' she said. 'Very funny.'

'You *are* very funny,' said Cal, grinning. 'Very, *very* funny.'

Other books by Claire Carmichael
Independent Readers (9+)

Dinosaurs in cyberspace, terrifying characters — Claire's clever and inventive sci-fi is scary and unputdownable.

Teenage Readers (12+)

Claire's outstanding ability to create future worlds where manufactured genetic beings have a society, and an underground group fights a silent war for personal privacy makes for thrilling reading.

Claire Carmichael's best-selling *Virtual Realities Trilogy* has been shortlisted for several children's choice awards. Claire is the author of many books for young readers, and (under another name) a celebrated author of detective novels for adults. She is an Australian but lives in Los Angeles, where she lectures in writing at UCLA. *Originator* and *Fabricant*, two action-packed and fascinating sci-fi novels for older readers, are listed as CBC notable books. *Fabricant* is also on the 2001 Western Australian Young Readers' Book Awards (Children's Choice award) list for older readers. Claire's latest sci-fi hit, *Incognito*, about loss of identity, makes fascinating reading.